Kiss Me in Carolina

||||| ||| ||||||| ||| ||||| |||
D1523124

By:

Brooke St. James

Other titles available from Brooke St. James:

Another Shot:
A Modern-Day Ruth and Boaz Story

When Lightning Strikes

Something of a Storm (All in Good Time #1)
Someone Someday (All in Good Time #2)

Finally My Forever (Meant for Me #1)
Finally My Heart's Desire (Meant for Me #2)
Finally My Happy Ending (Meant for Me #3)

Shot by Cupid's Arrow

Dreams of Us

Meet Me in Myrtle Beach (Hunt Family #1)

Prologue

Logan Ritchie made six million dollars in his most recent film role. He'd been acting since he was a child, and was now one of the most sought after leading men in Hollywood. His first big break was playing Taylor on Disney Channel's *Taylor and Tig*, which was a massive hit that ran for six seasons. Now, however, Logan took on much more serious roles in action and drama films. He was the tall, dark, handsome type who had the acting skills to back up his movie-star appearance—an A-lister who had more job offers than he could shake a stick at and walked the red carpet at all the major award shows.

Paparazzi, lights, and glamor aside, Logan was just a normal, down-to-earth guy who enjoyed hanging out with his friends and family. He was born in North Carolina, but at the age of five he told his parents that he wanted to be in movies, and they took him seriously. His dad, who worked for the USPS, applied for a transfer to California, and the rest, as they say, is history.

So, there he was, way out in Hollywood, living the dream. His extended family was still in North Carolina, but his mom, dad, and sister were all with him in Los Angeles, and he considered it his home. He lived in his own place, but it was close to the one he bought for his parents, and they saw each other all the time.

They lived in a gated Hollywood subdivision, but it wasn't as extravagant as Logan could have afforded. He had one car, not five, and he enjoyed the simple things in life. He usually had a bit of an entourage, but that was just because he'd rather have people around than be alone. His long-time best friends, Nico and Phillip, both had rooms at his house even though they technically didn't live there. He trusted them, and they took care of his dog, Sampson, when he was out of town, which was often.

Currently, Nico was sitting on the couch watching TV while Logan was in the kitchen talking to his mom and sister. Sampson, the professionally trained German Shepherd, was curled up on a rug next to Logan's feet.

"Is it that girl you met while we were in Myrtle Beach?" his mom, Denise, asked.

He nodded in answer to her question.

"The one you met at the party?"

He nodded again.

"What's her name again?"

"London," he said.

"Oh, yeah," Denise said. "I remember her telling that story about her parents conceiving her there."

Logan was silent for a few long seconds, wondering what he'd gotten himself into.

"London and Logan," Denise said. "That sort of has a ring to it, I guess."

"She's not my girlfriend, Mom."

Denise smirked at him. "Does she know that?"

"What's that supposed to mean?"

"It means what it sounds like. Does she think she's your girlfriend?"

He shrugged and absentmindedly rubbed Sampson's belly with his foot.

"Yes she does," Charlotte chimed in, without looking up from her phone. "Of course she does. Why else do you think she'd be coming here?"

"Well, have you been leading her to believe it?" Denise asked, studying her son.

He groaned as he stretched his arms toward the ceiling, clearly avoiding the question.

"Why are you being so weird about this?" she asked. "You're either dating her or your not. If you are, a visit should be a pleasant experience. If you're not, you should just tell her not to come."

He sighed, which made his mother glare at him. "What's going on, Logan?"

"Her dad's Charles Ryder."

Denise shrugged as if the name didn't mean anything to her.

"He's a big time entrepreneur on the East Coast," Logan said. "—a restaurant guy. He's not even a chef, he's a businessman, but every restaurant he opens turns into a gold mine."

"And you think he'll be a good contact if you want to eventually open a restaurant of your own," Denise said, reading between the lines of what her son was saying. Logan had mentioned the idea quite a few times, and she knew it was something he wanted to peruse eventually.

"He's not just a good contact, he's *the* contact. The only contact I'd need. If I want to open a restaurant, he's the guy who could help me do it right."

"So, basically he's just using the guy's daughter," Charlotte interjected, "which is fine when she's across the country and only requires a few texts a week, but now she's coming here, and he has to smile and act like he likes her in front of everyone."

Logan picked up a pen that was resting on the countertop and threw it at his sister, who was still staring down at her phone.

"Heyyyy," she said. "I'm just telling the truth."

"Yeah, but you make it sound like I'm trying to play her or something."

Charlotte narrowed her eyes at her brother. "What else is it called when you're talking to her because of her dad?"

"It's not like that."

"What's it like?"

"I like her and everything. She's a cool girl. I just don't need to be quote-unquote dating anyone right now. I have a lot going on."

"It is sort of a bad week," Denise said, trying to help him out with an excuse. "You have Cody and Paige coming in. Just tell her you'll have your cousin and his wife in from out of town."

"I already told her that," he said. "She's staying with a friend while she's here, so it doesn't really matter if I have company or not."

"How long's she staying?"

"I don't know—like ten days or something."

His mom gasped like that was much longer than she expected. "You're gonna be shooting in Santa Barbara during that time."

"I know."

"So just tell her you're gonna be busy."

"I already did. She said there's no pressure, she just wants to hook up when we can."

Denise shrugged. "I don't know why you're asking my advice, Logan. It sounds like you've got it all figured out. Just see her when you can, I guess."

"I thought maybe you and Charlotte could hang out with her a little bit," he said.

"I'll take her shopping if I'm using your credit card," Charlotte volunteered.

Denise shot her a motherly glare. "Nobody's taking anybody shopping," she said. "We'll have you guys over for dinner if you want us to meet her."

"You already met her," he said.

"You know what I mean."

"I'll take her shopping," Charlotte mouthed behind her mom's back. Logan winked at her, and she winked back.

"I just don't know if it's a good idea to lead her on, though, baby."

"I knew you were gonna say that," Logan said.

"Then obviously you see the flaws in your plan."

"There's no plan, Mom. I just don't want to call it off with her quite yet. It's not just about her dad. I think she's okay, too."

"Just not okay enough to date her if her dad wasn't who he is."

He sighed. "It's good to surround yourself with successful people. Her dad's a factor, I'm not gonna lie. But that might be because I don't know her that well yet. Who knows, maybe she'll come over here, and I'll fall in love with her and not even care that her dad is a ki-jillionaire, genius, restaurant guy."

Denise sighed. "You better end it sooner rather than later if you figure out she's not right for you, Logan. I have a feeling you'd rather this guy see you as a someone who was once friends with his daughter than the guy who led her on and broke her heart."

"I'm not leading her on," he said, smiling. "We might still fall in love."

"I'm pretty sure she's already there," Charlotte said.

Logan continued to smile as he shook his head, telling them he had everything under control. "She's cool," he said. "She's not asking me about commitment or anything. She's independent. She's just coming to visit her friend, and she wants to try to see me if possible."

Denise shrugged. "Sounds like you've got it all figured out."

"I guess I just wanted you guys to know she'd be around."

"Are you gonna take her on the set?" Denise asked.

"I probably will."

"You know they'll photograph you together," she warned. "And they're gonna speculate on her being your girlfriend."

He nodded.

"And you're okay with that?"

"It's fine, Mom. You're making it more of a big deal than it is. It's not like it's my first time to hang out with a girl."

"All right," she said. "I'll quit asking questions."

"I really don't know what to expect, to tell you the truth. I'll probably hang out with her a few times, and before you know it, the week will be over."

"Famous last words," Charlotte said.

Logan ignored his sister's comment, and dug in the fridge for the carton of orange juice. He unscrewed the cap and took a gulp directly from the container before setting it back in its place.

"Where are Cody and Paige staying?" Charlotte asked, changing the subject.

"Upstairs," Logan said.

"I want to stay over when they're here so I can hang out with Paige."

"You can," he said. "You should just move in for the next couple of weeks so you can be here through London's trip, too."

That sounded like a great idea to Charlotte since Logan would no doubt spoil her. She smiled and lifted her eyebrows at her mom.

"What about school?" Denise asked, practically.

"I'll still go to my classes," she said.

Denise made it obvious by her nonchalant facial expression that she didn't care either way about the matter. Charlotte had, more than once, brought up moving in with Logan permanently, so a two-week visit wasn't necessarily big news.

"Whatever you two work out is fine."

Chapter 1

My heart sank, and a feeling of dread washed over me. "I have absolutely no desire to have her stay with me, Mom."

My mom, who I could see through Skype on my computer, laughed and shook her head at me. "You don't really have a choice, Rachel." She wrinkled her nose. "I shouldn't say it like that. You do have a choice, but I'm asking you to please consider letting her stay with you while she's in town. Her dad is our most faithful supporter."

I had nothing in common with London Ryder. We were the opposite of compatible. I'd met her on several occasions when we were younger, but hadn't seen her in years.

"Why's she coming here? I know it's not to see me."

"She's got a boyfriend in L.A."

"Can't she stay with him?" I asked.

My mother leveled me with that strict, motherly stare that said I should be ashamed of myself for asking if a girl could stay with her boyfriend when that implied they'd be spending the night together.

"Can't she get a hotel?" I amended. "Her dad probably owns one she could stay in."

"She's asked specifically if she could stay with you. Her dad contacted me personally."

I scrunched up my face at my mom, joking with her about my reluctant agreement.

She smiled. "Thank you."

"How long's she staying?"

"Ten days."

"*Ten days*? Are you serious? I thought you were gonna say three—four tops."

"Don't worry, it'll go by fast. She's got that boyfriend, and you've got school. I'm sure you'll barely even know she's there."

"I hope she's not expecting me to show her around or anything."

"She's not. I already told her dad you were in school."

"Did you tell him I said I'd do it?"

"No, sweetheart, I didn't. I wanted to leave that up to you. I told him I'd check with you to make sure you had room, but warned him that even if you did, you'd be busy with school." She sighed and smiled at me. "I'm sure you'll barely even know she's there."

I couldn't even imagine what it would be like to have London at my apartment for a whole ten days.

"I think her boyfriend's some famous actor," my mom added as if that might make me feel better about it.

"Of course he is," I said. "And I'll hear all about how glamorous it is."

My mom tilted her head and smiled patiently. "Why don't you try to make the most of it? Like you said, you haven't seen her in years. Maybe things

13

have changed. Maybe you'll have more in common now."

"Maybe."

"And if you don't, you'll still be a gracious host, because that's just how you are."

I cracked a smile. "You're probably right, but I still get to complain to you about it, don't I?"

She smiled. "You can complain to me all you want, sweetheart."

***

A week later, London Ryder arrived at LAX, and who do you think was there to pick her up? Me. I put a little thought into what I was wearing simply because I didn't want her to ask me why I didn't. Yep. She was the type of girl who would say, "*If you'd fix yourself up a little bit, you'd be pretty*," and other lovely things like that. I was about fifteen the last time I saw her, and those types of sentiments flowed from her lips the entire time we were together. She was an entitled, southern debutante type who thought her accent was charming and looked down her nose at me. I could only hope things would be different now that we were older.

I stood at baggage claim, watching as passengers on her flight came down the escalators, telling myself over and over again that her dad's contributions kept my parents' center afloat.

There was no mistaking her when she came into view. She was dressed to the nines in chic clothes, looking like an Urban Outfitters ad. She had enough gold necklaces and bracelets to feed an entire country. I knew it was real gold, too. She wasn't a knock-off jewelry type of person.

"Oh my goodness, Rachel Stephens, you look so good!" she said in her slow, southern drawl as she drew me in for a hug. She went in for the kiss on each of my cheeks, and I tried not to be too awkward about going through the motions with her. It was so weird to hear that accent coming out of someone named London. I remember thinking that when we were little—wondering why she didn't have a British accent. I smiled inwardly at the thought.

"Thank you," I said after we exchanged fake kisses. "You look great, too. It's been forever."

"More than ten years, I think. I remember because that last time I saw you, I was about to get my first car. That was the BMW, so I was only fifteen. Can you believe how time flies?" She reached out and touched the long, dark hair that hung over my shoulder. "I can't believe you wear your hair so dark like this in Los Angeles. Doesn't it get hot?"

I shook my head and smiled.

"I thought everybody out west was supposed to be blonde," she said.

I had no idea how to respond. She was saying it in an almost accusatory way like I was doing something wrong by having dark hair, and it left me speechless. I smiled as genuinely as I could. "I can't believe you're here!" I said. I pointed to the baggage belt. "I guess we should look for your luggage."

"I have three bags."

"Oh, okay."

I stepped closer to the conveyer belt, which was moving, but was still empty where we were standing. I stared at it even though it was empty and I had no idea what I was looking for. I looked at it simply to avoid looking at her. *Lord, please help me to be positive. Help me to like this girl, Amen.*

"One of them's pretty much empty," she said. I figured you'd be taking me shopping while I'm here."

"Oh, did your dad tell you I'm really busy with school? I just started my last year, and I can't really miss."

"Yeah." She gave me a slow wink. "But I'm sure you'll have some time to do a little shopping, right?"

I knew she assumed the idea would be tempting to me, but shopping was seriously one of my most hated past times. I didn't even like to do it for normal things like jeans, and shirts, and shoes, and underwear, much less go from store to store looking for items you didn't even need—browsing, so to speak. I did my best not to cringe at the idea of going with her. "I'm sure we can figure something out for the weekend if you haven't already gone without me by then," I said, trying to be nice without officially committing to a shopping trip.

The luggage had just begun to come past us, and I motioned for her to look at it since she was now digging in her purse and didn't seem interested in trying to find her bags.

"I'll see it when it comes," she said. "You can't miss it." Without looking up, she said, "Dad said you're in school to be a dentist."

"I am."

"And you just started your last year?"

"Yep." I kept my eyes on the belt for something I '*couldn't miss*,' but didn't see anything.

London continued digging in her purse. "That's pretty impressive. How long does it take to become a dentist?"

"Eight years."

"Eight?" she asked, finally looking up from her purse with wide eyes. "That's forever. How'd you even do that? Are you old enough to have had eight years of school."

"I started some of my undergraduate stuff a little early," I said. "Since I was homeschooled."

"Oh, yeah," she said, as if the word homeschool was just another reminder of how weird and sheltered I was. "Are you moving to Kenya when you're done?"

I could tell she was proud of herself for knowing where my parents' school was. She smiled as if she had done a good deed simply by remembering.

"No. Not full time at least. I'll visit regularly, but I told my parents years ago that I wasn't cut out for fulltime missionary life. I'm much better suited for living here and making routine trips."

"What about your parents?" she asked. "Ooh, there's one of mine," she added, pointing to the lipstick-red piece of luggage making it's way toward us. I stooped to pick it up and set it near my feet before scanning the rest of the belt for anything bright red. I didn't see anything right away.

"What about them?" I asked, referring to her vague question about my parents.

"Are they just planning staying in Kenya for the rest of their lives?"

"Probably so," I said. "They make trips back to the states to see me and for fundraising or whatever, but they're pretty wrapped up in the projects they have going on. They have three locations now. It's really grown into something more massive than they ever expected. That's one of the main reasons I chose dentistry. I plan on going back at least twice a year for dental clinics. So many people need procedures, and have no access to that."

"What about your brother?" she asked. "Don't you have a brother?"

I nodded. "He's still in Kenya with my parents for now, but he talks about coming to the states."

"What's his name?"

"Cub."

"That's a crazy name," she said.

"It's a nickname."

"What's it short for?"

"It's not short for anything."

"What's his real name?"

"William. But no one ever uses it. I had to think about it just now when you asked."

She smiled and stared off into space as if imagining something. "I remember him," she said, nodding as her smile grew. "He was cute, wasn't he?"

I shrugged. "Hard to say since he's my bother."

She laughed and pushed at my shoulder. "Aw, come on. If I had a brother I'd totally know if he was hot or not. He's fine and you know it."

"If you say so," I said, shrugging.

"Are you gonna live in L.A. when you graduate?" she asked.

"I'm planning on it since the rest of my family lives here—aunts, and uncles, and stuff. I have a job set up at an upscale pediatric practice. I'll work there a few times a week with the main goal to support my free clinics in the city and trips to Kenya."

She nodded distractedly as if she didn't hear a word I said, and then pointed to another bright red piece of luggage.

I bent to pick it up as it came past. I groaned with the effort. This one was definitely heavier than the last. London was standing right on top of me when I straightened, and I flinched and stared at her wondering what she was doing.

"I think that's Ryan Seacrest over there," she whispered frantically. She flashed me her teeth. "Do I have anything?" she asked.

"Any what?"

"Anything between my teeth—or lipstick on them or anything. Do I look good?"

"You look great," I said. "Nothing's on your teeth."

She smiled as she used her tongue to wipe them, just in case.

"Oh my gosh, I can't believe I've only been here five minutes and I'm already seeing Ryan Seacrest!" She watched as the guy in question walked past without stopping at baggage claim.

"Is this one yours?" I asked, pointing at another bright red bag coming down the line.

She glanced at it just long enough to nod before looking at Ryan Seacrest's back. She let out a wistful sigh. "I love Los Angeles already," she said. "I might just have to move here."

I coughed to keep myself from making some other disapproving noise. I thought it was a little peculiar that she was star struck over Ryan Seacrest when her boyfriend was some huge movie star, but I obviously didn't mention it. I didn't really care. I knew, based on first impressions, that she hadn't changed a bit, I could see it in the way she looked at me. It was like she pitied me for being me, which was funny because I sort of felt the same way about her. My plan was to smile and be as friendly and forgiving as possible. I knew my mom needed her dad, so the least I could do was be cordial for the next ten days. *What was ten days in the grand scheme of things, anyway?*

London's flight had arrived late that afternoon, so by the time we unpacked her things, straightened out some business with the car, and got some dinner, it was just about time for me to turn in. I told her I had some notes to look over before my clinicals the following day, which was not only the truth, but also a convenient excuse to head to my room early. London was so obsessed with trying to contact her boyfriend that she didn't even really hear what I was saying when I told her I was going to bed.

I opened my laptop and composed an email to my mother.

Greetings from California. Just your favorite daughter checking in to remind you I'm a rockstar for agreeing to host this lovely houseguest. I'll survive, but it'll be hard. She has already tried to talk me into receiving a Botox treatment while she was here. I asked her why she thought I needed it, and she pinched my forehead and told me those lines were only getting deeper. "It's preventative," she said. "Everyone should start getting it at 25." She also gave me a big speech about watching my carbs and what types of clothes would be "more becoming" on me. She has decided that my car isn't good enough for her to be seen in, so her father has rented us a Mercedes convertible. She says I'm to drive it since I know my way around. I assume that makes me her chauffeur, which is not so bad, since it's a super nice car. I didn't even know it was possible to rent a car like that. Tell Cub he'd be jealous. You were right about her boyfriend. He's a mega movie star. Even I recognize his name. The only problem is that London can't seem to reach him. She's tried all afternoon. Makes me wonder if she knows him at all. She is a piece of work. She asks questions and then doesn't pay attention to my answers. She is much prettier and taller than I remember, but her personality is exactly the same. Please pray for me.

Your faithful daughter,
Rachel

I deleted it without pressing send.

My mom would find the humor in it, but she didn't need the weight of worrying about my problems. And it wasn't really a problem anyway— not compared to most of the world's issues. It felt good simply to type out my gripes and then erase them, which was exactly what I did.

Chapter 2

We were now four days into London's trip. Forty percent over—only a little over half to go, and honestly, it hadn't been all that bad. I'd been busy with school and wasn't even home during the day. She was so obsessed with contacting her boyfriend that she hardly noticed me anyway. I just went about my business.

It was late Friday afternoon, and there was a note on the table when I came into my apartment after clinicals. It was from London saying that she was spending the day with her boyfriend and that she didn't know what time she'd be back.

I smiled thinking about eating some carbs without her sitting there judging me. *Pizza? Thai food? The possibilities were endless. I should call it in soon before she gets back.*

I was exhausted from a long week at school, and by 7PM, I had on my pajamas. I was sitting on the couch eating a big box of noodle-y Pad Thai without a care in the world when London came back. She twirled around my living room like a little trendy-looking tornado. She was on cloud nine, or cloud thirty-seven—somewhere way out there in the stratosphere. I couldn't help but smile at how uninhibited she was. It was somewhat cute... in a sad sort of way. She danced and giggled like a kid at Christmas. She didn't even notice my Thai food nor did she notice my old pajamas. I decided I quite liked the effect Logan Ritchie had on London. She wiggled and jiggled and kept saying things like, "*That was crazy,*" and "*I can't believe it,*" so much that when she finally started telling me the story, I didn't think it quite lived up to the hype.

"He had like *five people* staying at his house," she said, still beaming. "That's why he's been so busy." She breathed deeply several times. She was completely out of breath as she relayed the story, and I didn't know if it was from nerves or from having danced around.

"Does he always have so many?" I asked as she caught her breath. I didn't really care; I was just trying to be nice.

"He usually just has a couple," she said. "His cousin, Cody, just got married and he brought his wife over here to see Hollywood. She'd never even been on a plane until a few weeks ago when they went on their honeymoon. I met them in Myrtle Beach the same weekend that I met Logan. They're really sweet. His sister, Charlotte, is also staying with him. You know, as company for Cody's wife while they're in town. They're leaving tomorrow, though. I don't know if Charlotte will stay, but Cody and Paige are headed back to Charlotte where they're from. They were only here for a few days. You should have seen the paparazzi following us today. It was crazy! We went out to eat lunch, and they were going nuts trying to get a photo of us. Logan's working this weekend. Until Monday, actually. He's starting a new movie, and they're filming a scene in Santa Barbra. He was saying—"

I held up a hand and stopped her in mid-sentence. "London, you have to slow down. You are talking like you had about twenty cups of coffee. I'm trying my best to follow what you're saying, but I was pretty much lost way back there when you were talking about his cousins. I think you mentioned someone named Charlotte, or the town Charlotte, or both. I also heard something about his cousin never flying on an airplane before, but that's about it."

London let out a long sigh as if trying to encourage herself to slowdown. "Basically, what I'm saying is that Logan's leaving tomorrow to spend the weekend in Santa Barbara. It's only an hour and a half away, but he's gonna spend two nights there so he doesn't have to commute."

She was super-excitable, and I still wasn't sure why. I smiled and nodded, but London was speaking so quickly that I could hardly understand her, and none of it really pertained to me anyway.

"He wants me to go over there with him!" she said. Her eyes looked as if they might bulge right out of her head. "He's staying in his trailer, but I'm just gonna get a hotel." She paused and stared at me. "And by I, I mean we." She bit her lip and gave me puppy dog eyes.

"Did you just say you wanted me to leave town with you?"

She nodded expectantly.

"For three days?"

"Just two nights. Saturday and Sunday. Couldn't you just skip school on Monday? Just one day while I'm here? It's all I ask!" She batted her eyes at me, and leaned against me like we were the best of friends. "Pleeease go with me!" she begged. "I really need you!"

"Why?" I asked, feeling genuinely confused.

"Because Logan said I should bring you. He said he'd be busy most of the day, and that I should bring my friend to keep me company. I knew you wouldn't want to do it, so I asked his sister, but she had other plans. You're my only hope!"

I tried to imagine what it would be like staying in a hotel room with London. *Could I do it?* "Just because he recommended you bring me doesn't mean you have to," I said. "Can't you just say I had work to do for school and you decided to come alone?"

"I don't want to do that," she said. "I sort of told him I was mostly here to see you and not him—you know, to make him a little jealous or whatever. So he sort of thinks I wouldn't want to go without having you with me."

"I thought you just said you asked his sister about going," I said.

"That has nothing to do with it," she said, looking at me like I was crazy.

I just sat there, trying to understand what she was saying. I wasn't well versed in relationship games, but apparently she was. I wondered, and not for the first time, if they were dating at all. I had already planned on taking Monday off. It was the easiest day for me to rearrange, and I figured I should show at least a little effort to hang out with her before she had to leave. "I already thought about taking Monday off," I said. "I thought we could have lunch with the guy I'm sort of seeing, and then I'd take you to a few shops."

"It would seriously mean everything to me if you decided to come to Santa Barbara instead," she said.

It was obvious that she was completely desperate for me to agree.

"Okay," I said.

Her face lit up. "Really? Are you serious?"

I nodded. "I'll take Monday off, but we need to get back at a reasonable hour. I need to be there early on Tuesday."

"Whatever you need," she said. "Oh, my gosh, I love you Rachel! Thank you so, so, so, so, so, much! You're awesome. We're gonna get you some good clothes to wear while we're there."

I cocked my head at her.

"I'm totally kidding!" she said. "I love your clothes. Your clothes are fine." She squealed. "I've got to pack! I'm so excited! You should be excited, too. Who knows who we're gonna get to meet!"

27

I smiled. "I can't wait," I said. It was partially true. I wasn't completely immune to the charms of pop culture, and to be honest, I was looking forward to seeing the process of filming a movie. I knew it'd be interesting to see how the whole thing worked. I *assumed* we'd be allowed to see some of it. Maybe not, maybe she'd drag me over there, and it would be a closed set, forcing us to hang out in the hotel room for most of the day while I talked her out of feeling desperate about not seeing Logan more. After a brief reminder to myself to think positive, I decided to assume the best.

We left Saturday morning at 10, and got to our hotel just before noon. I halfway expected London to ask me to split the room with her, and I was prepared to do so, but she didn't. She just handed the clerk her father's credit card without even looking at the price.

She was a mini-bar user, too. Within minutes of walking in the door, she opened a bottled water and three granola bars. She only took one tiny bite off each one before deciding she didn't like any of them, and throwing them all away. I knew it must cost an arm and a leg for those items in a place like this, and I did my best not to judge her for being wasteful. After growing up in Kenya with those kids my parents rescued, I had a hard time watching anyone throw away money.

But really, who was I to judge, right? Her dad had been extremely generous with my parents over the years. Besides, it wasn't my place to worry about

28

what other people did with their money. I made a conscious effort not to let it bug me. As conservative as I thought I was, there were bound to be people in the world who would consider me wasteful. My mom would say, "Don't point your finger, because you've got three pointing back at you." I smiled, thinking about my mother.

London and I were staying in a one-bedroom suite, so she moved her things into the bedroom while I got situated near the couch.

"I've been in there texting Logan," she announced about thirty minutes later when she came back into the living area.

She was beaming.

I'd been reading an email from one of my professors, so I was thrown off by her enthusiasm. "Don't act so excited," she said, looking annoyed.

I smiled. "I'm sorry, I was just thinking about something else when you came in. Did you say you've been talking to Logan?"

"Yes."

She gave me a wide-eyed serious expression. I knew she was expecting me to react a certain way, but I wasn't exactly sure what that way was.

I smiled and shook my fists slightly. "Yayyy!" I said, hoping for the best.

She rolled her eyes and groaned. "I can't believe you don't even care about any of this. You're gonna get to see a scene from a movie being filmed. Not a made for TV movie, but a real, silver-screen movie.

You can't be in it or anything. I was asking Logan if I could be an extra or whatever, but he said they already had people doing that. Apparently, there's gonna be a lot of people involved since it's a bar scene. He said we had to stay out of the way, and I told him we'd be totally invisible. They're shooting some inside the bar this afternoon, but they have to wait till the sun goes down to film the part where the scene moves outside." She paused and looked me over before adding, "What are you gonna wear?"

I looked down at my clothes. I was wearing skinny jeans, a pair of light pink, low-top Chuck Taylors and an off-the-shoulder sweater I picked up at a consignment shop. It was pretty much my favorite outfit. In other words, I had already considered what I was wearing, and this was it. This was my *I put some thought into what I'm wearing* outfit.

"I figured I'd wear this," I said. "What are you wearing?"

"I have a dress if you want to try it on."

I sucked air through the cracks in my clinched teeth, making a sound of reluctance. "I'm not really a dress kind of girl. Thanks anyway."

She squinted at me. "What do you mean? What do you wear to church?"

"Jeans." I shrugged. "I mean, I guess I have a few skirts or whatever, but usually I just try to wear jeans if I can help it." I gestured at her phone. "Did he say there's a dress code or something?"

She let out a frustrated sigh. "No, he didn't say there's a dress code. It's just respectful to clean yourself up. It's nice manners to dress well."

I looked down at my clothes. "I like this outfit. It's one of my favorites." I smelled my armpit. "And I smell good. I just took a shower this morning. In my book, I *am* cleaned up."

She threw her hands up. "Do whatever you want," she said. "Just don't blame me if I get to be an extra and you don't."

"I promise I won't blame you for that," I said, stifling a smile. "You can go be an extra all day long. I'll cheer for you from the sidelines."

"Please don't cheer, Rachel," she said in all seriousness. "Logan specifically said we need to be quiet and try to stay out of the way."

I stared at her, unable to believe that she, in her southern drawl, was mothering me as if I was about to go out of control on set.

"It was a figure of speech," I said. "I wasn't really going to cheer. I know we need to stay out of the way."

I picked up the paperback novel that was on the seat next to me. "That's why I'm bringing this. I'm sure we'll be lucky if we can even get close enough to see what's going on."

London studied me for a few seconds. "Well, I guess just wear whatever you want then," she said, looking down her nose at me.

I smiled. "Thanks," I said. "I will."

She flashed me an overly-sweet, fake smile before heading toward her room again. "Suit yourself," she said shrugging as she walked away. "We're gonna be leaving here in about an hour."

"I'm ready when you are," I said, knowing that would push her buttons.

She didn't bother responding.

Chapter 3

The scene was being filmed at a bar on the outskirts of town. It was up on a hillside, and had a beautiful view of the city and ocean. I'd been living in L.A. since I was 17, and I'd never been to Santa Barbara. I decided I liked it, and would return some other time without London.

There were vehicles parked along the side of the road as we approached, and I pulled her rented Mercedes behind one of them. "What are you doing?" she asked, looking at me as if I was crazy.

I gestured at the car in front of me. "I'm parking."

She looked at the GPS on the dash. "The address says it's way up there."

"I know, but everybody seems to be parking right here." I motioned again to the parked car in front of me. "I'm sure they have the actual parking lot barricaded off since they're filming a scene right there."

She rolled down her window and craned her neck out to try to see down the street. "I think we can get closer than this," she said. "Don't you?"

"Not really, or I wouldn't have parked here. But I'll drive you up there if you want."

"I do," she said, without hesitation.

I pulled onto the road and slowly approached the address. We passed about thirty cars before making our way to the driveway, which was blocked off. The building was set back off the road a little ways, but we could see it, along with people, trailers, cameras, and tons of other equipment. It was exciting.

"Dang," she said, dazedly. Then she smiled at me. "How about you just drop me off?"

I didn't mind that idea at all. In fact, I'd probably take my time parking the car and walking back up there. I smiled. "Sure," I said. I pulled into the driveway just far enough to turn around and head back the way I came.

It took about fifteen minutes for me to make my way back to the entrance on foot, and I approached tentatively since I technically had no business being there. There were tons of people milling around the outskirts of the parking lot, but I couldn't seem to locate London.

"I'm sorry ma'am, it's a closed set if you don't have one of these," a man said. He had approached from the side of me, so I was caught off guard, which made me instantly nervous and probably suspicious looking. I turned to face him with a smile that I hoped seemed natural. He was holding up some sort of card that was hanging around his neck by a lanyard.

"I'm, uh, here with my friend who's here with Logan Ritchie. I think I'm maybe supposed to have one of those," I said, almost apologetically.

"She's with me," I heard London call from a distance.

We both turned to find her approaching with a lanyard around her neck and another in her hand. There was a guy walking with her, but I knew it wasn't Logan Ritchie—unless he had a ton of makeup on and had lost about fifty pounds. The person walking with her was a super skinny Asian guy. He was dressed in all black, high fashion clothes, and he walked with a purpose.

London pulled back when I shifted my attention to her. She pointed at the Asian guy's back with an intense expression on her face and mouthed some words to me. It wasn't just one word, either. She was trying to make me discern a whole sentence. She must have thought I was a champion lip reader or something. I just made a confused expression that said I wasn't even *close* to understanding what she was saying. She quit trying and rolled her eyes at me.

The guy in black crossed to say something to the person who'd been questioning me, and London marched right up to me. "He can make me an extra!" she whispered frantically. It was all she had time to get out before the guy in black finished what he was saying to the questioner and came to stand with us.

"Are you ready?" he asked in a no-nonsense way, staring at London.

"I'm gonna run an errand with Kai," she informed me. "The director forgot something and we have to pick it up." She smiled at Kai. "Kai's the director's assistant," she said proudly in that slow, sweet, southern accent. She shifted her attention to me and handed me the extra lanyard. "I told him you would just sit in the picnic area and not bother anybody."

I grabbed the lanyard with the same hand that I was using to hold my book. I took it between two of my fingers and then wiggled the whole handful at her. "Nobody will even know I'm here," I said, smiling.

"We better go," he said.

"I have a convertible if you want to take that," she said.

Kai cocked his head at her as if considering the possibilities.

She pointed at me, searching me with her eyes for the keys. "It's a Mercedes. We just pulled up here and turned around in it a little while ago. It's super nice. It's brand new."

"Can I drive it?" he asked, smiling for the first time at the thought.

She beamed at his enthusiasm. I could tell she loved the idea of pleasing him, especially when he evidently had the power to make her an extra in the movie.

"You most certainly can!" She snapped her fingers at me. "She has the keys," she said, still smiling at Kai. I fished into my back pocket and pulled them out.

Kai reached out for them, but she put out a hand to stop him and smiled at me. "Would you mind bringing it around for us?" she asked, in a syrupy sweet tone. She gave me pleading eyes. "Neither of us wore good shoes for walking down that big hill."

"We can walk," Kai said.

"She doesn't mind, and it'll only take her a minute," London said. She pointed at my shoes. "She has her sneakers on."

"I don't mind," I said, before Kai had the chance to refuse again. I took off toward the car at a faster pace than when I was on my way up there a few minutes earlier. Part of me felt embarrassed that London had treated me like her valet in front of that guy, but the other part of me was just glad to be rid of her for a little while, and was happy to bring them the car if it meant she'd be disappearing in it.

I pulled into the driveway and got out of the car, handing the keys to Kai. He had the decency to thank me when he took them out of my hand.

"Logan's in a meeting," London said in that same warning, motherly tone she'd been using earlier. "So don't try to look for him or anything. You'll find the picnic area past those trailers. Just stay over there out of the way."

I picked up my book and shot her a smile that was likely not sincere at all. "Thanks," I said.

She smiled. "Have fun!"

"You too," I said as I turned to walk away.

She and Kai were both making giddy exclamations as they sat in the car. I didn't look back, but I could hear them.

The picnic area was easy to find. It was a huge tent set up on the far side of the trailers. I thought people might question my presence, but no one seemed to notice me. A few people glanced at me, but we just smiled like we assumed each other should be there. There were ten or fifteen picnic tables lined up underneath the tent, but it was a beautiful day, so some people were scattered around outside the tent in the nearby grass and woods.

I almost went directly into the woods, but I decided to try to find a spot at one of the picnic tables since I promised London that I'd stay there. All of the tables were occupied, but a few of them only had a couple of people. I went to one of the tables that was sparsely occupied, and stood at the empty end of it. There were two people sitting at the other end having a conversation. The tables were huge, and there was no way I could hear what they were saying, so I assumed they wouldn't mind if I took a seat on the far end. I carefully sat on the very edge of the bench, which made them both look at me.

"Do you guys mind if I sit here?" I asked.

I held up my book, indicating that I'd be busy doing my own thing and wouldn't pay attention to them.

They looked at each other before looking back at me in a reluctant but snobby way. "We're kind of having a private conversation right now," one of them said slowly.

What followed was the most awkward ten seconds of my life, even more awkward than London treating me like her servant. I smiled like I thought they were joking, but they didn't smile back. The tables were huge, and there was no way I could hear them. I wasn't even interested in hearing them. I quickly realized they were dead serious. They were telling me I couldn't sit there. Wow. My heart started racing, and blood rose to my cheeks. I hated confrontations—especially really embarrassing ones. I was already sitting down by the time what they were saying sunk in, and I got back to my feet, feeling a bit like I was in a dream. *Forget this...* There was no way I was trying another table.

I numbly made my way out of the tent to the wooded area nearby. I'd sit by a tree. Trees never told anyone they were having a private conversation. I found a perfect spot near a tree with a flat rock just big enough for me to sit comfortably.

"Looks like you got a good spot," I heard a guy's voice say from behind me as I dusted off the rock. I turned to find Logan Ritchie smiling at me.

I was still all shook up from the table snobs, and his presence had me feeling breathless. He was wearing khakis and a vintage black T-shirt with a few stripes across the chest. He had on skater shoes, and I caught myself wondering if that was his wardrobe for the movie or his own clothes. *What had he even said, anyway?*

"I'm sorry, what?" I asked as calmly as I could.

Every second felt like a lifetime. I had all sorts of thoughts, one after another. *Don't stare, just smile, act natural, that's Logan Ritchie standing right there in front of you. He's just a regular guy—a normal guy, like your brother.*

His smile broadened at what I assumed was my stunned expression. *Snap out of it*, I told myself.

"I said it looks like you got the best seat in the house up here," he said. He pointed at me with a casual flick of his hand. "I saw you under the tent. I was trying to catch up with you, but you ran up here."

"I ran?" I asked.

He smiled and shrugged. "You walked quickly," he said. "And I was by my trailer when I first saw you, so I had some catching up to do.

I stared at him, wondering the obvious. "You might have me confused with someone else," I said. "Because we've never met."

"I assumed you were Rachel," he said. He pointed at my shirt, and I looked down to find the lanyard. "They're color coded to tell why you're here. All my guests have the green ones. That tells me you're here with me, so I did the math."

He was still smiling. It was so warm and inviting that I smiled right back at him. His was the friendliest face I'd seen so far on the set, and I was thankful for the warm welcome.

Logan was much better looking in person than he was in movies. Talk about brown eyes that could look straight through you. Maybe it was just that being himself looked good on him. I smiled at the thought that even though I'd seen him in a few movies, I'd never seen the real him. The guy standing in front of me was the *real* Logan Ritchie, and I was instantly drawn to him. I felt no need to explain my presence or that I would be quiet and stay out of the way. His smile told me I didn't need to bother with that stuff.

"What are you smiling at?" he asked.

"I was just thinking about all the characters you've played, and how this one's just the plain old you."

He held out his hands. "I'm playing me right now," he said, smiling.

"You seem nice," I said.

"So do you." He held eye contact with me for a long while after that, so long that I finally broke it and glanced at my feet before looking at him again with a smile.

"I thought London would be with you," he said.

"She ran an errand with the director's assistant," I said. "I think she thought you'd be tied up for a while. She's gonna be sad she missed you."

"She's the one who's gonna be tied up," he said.

"Why's that?"

"Because Kai had to go back to L.A. to pick up something John left behind."

"Back to L.A.?" I asked.

He smiled. "Yeah."

"I don't think London knew that," I said.

He shrugged. "They'll probably be gone for four or five hours depending on traffic."

I put my hand over my mouth, wondering how London would react when she found out. I had to think she wouldn't be pleased, but one never knew with that girl.

"You wanna go for a walk?" he asked.

I was lost in thought about London, and his question made me tilt my head at him. "Me?"

He smiled. "Yeah."

"I was just planning on reading a little bit."

"You got something against walks?" he asked with a teasing grin.

I smiled. "Not really, I just promised I'd stay out of the way. I'm good just sitting here reading. You don't need to entertain me or anything. I know you have work to do."

"I'm actually just trying to entertain myself," he said, looking around. "We can't do anything until Kai gets back with John's stuff. That's what our meeting was about."

"So you're set back four or five hours?" I asked.

He let out a humorless laugh as he stretched. "That's nothing. We have delays all the time. My whole life's a series of delays."

I smiled and squinted at him. "Somehow I doubt that."

He let out a final groan as he finished his stretch. His shirt had come up while his arms were in the air, exposing the bottom portion of his perfect male abdomen. I tried not to look, but it was literally impossible. I had to squeeze in a tiny glance.

"You're life's pretty exciting, too, from what I hear," he said. He smiled at me and I answered with a confused expression that made him continue. "London told us all about you when we were at lunch the other day."

"She did?" I asked. My expression must have been comically confused because Logan laughed. "She said your parents were missionaries and you grew up helping them in their orphanage. Now you're a dentist and you're saving the world in your spare time. She thinks the world of you."

"She said all that?" I asked, feeling like I was in some other reality. I was staring blankly at his face, trying to associate the London I knew with the one who said all those kind things about me.

"I feel like I should brush my teeth right now," he said, using his hand to shield his mouth.

"Because I'm a dentist?" I asked, smiling.

"Yeah," he said. "It's kind of intimidating."

"Well, here's two things to make you feel better… one is that I'm not quite a dentist yet. I still have a few months to go, and two, you're teeth are obviously perfect. You get an A-plus from me on first impressions."

He had dropped his hand, and I could clearly see his teeth as he smiled.

I shook my head. "They're literally perfect," I said, inspecting them. "I'm a fan of your work."

He cracked up laughing at that. "You're a fan of my teeth-brushing skills?" he asked.

I nodded and smiled.

"I have to say, that's a first."

Chapter 4

I was standing in a fairly secluded area talking to Logan for about five minutes before a guy walked up to us. He had on a green lanyard that was exactly the same as mine, so I deduced that he, like me, was here as a guest of Logan.

"What are you doing?" he asked Logan in a matter of fact tone.

Logan gestured to me. "I'm talking."

The guy looked me over as if trying to figure out who I was.

"Nico, this is Rachel, she's London's friend," Logan said.

I had the strong urge to defend myself by saying something like, "We're not really all that close," but I didn't. I knew that would be rude—especially after she apparently up-sold me already. I just smiled and waved, and Nico returned the gesture before shifting his attention to Logan again.

"What do you wanna do for the next few hours?" Nico asked.

"I'd like to stay out here and get some fresh air since it's so nice," Logan said, gesturing around him to indicate their surroundings.

"I'm probably just gonna hang out with Phillip in the trailer."

"Why'd you come out here then?" Logan asked in that teasing way guys who are good friends talk to each other.

Nico shrugged. "Cuz I thought you might want to go somewhere since you have a break."

"I'm good," Logan said. He looked at me. "Unless you want to go somewhere."

I put a hand to my chest instinctually. "Me?"

He looked over my shoulder at the empty space behind me, giving me a hard time. I smiled at his silliness, but shook my head in answer to his question. "I'll probably just hang out over here and read, unless I'm needed for something else."

Logan's wide mouth curved upward in an easy, confident grin. It was no wonder he was a famous movie star. He had that extra something. Magnetism. "I believe you *are* needed for something else," he said, seeming entertained.

"What is it?"

"A walk with me."

"A walk?" Nico asked, seeming bored. He turned and waved at us. "I'll be in the trailer if you need me."

"Nice meeting you!" I called.

He turned and smiled. "You too."

Logan looked at me. "So?"

"So what?"

"You coming?"

"Are you sure you want to…" I trailed off, not really knowing what I wanted to ask.

"Why don't you want to take a walk with me?" I glanced over his shoulder at the groups of people standing around. "I just didn't know if you could take a walk. You know with everything going on here and stuff."

He laughed, which made me look at him. Our eyes locked as he continued smiling. "I'm the one who works here," he said. "I know when I have to be back."

I glanced at the wooded hillside and then past the movie commotion toward the street. "Where do you want to walk?" I asked.

He gestured to the wooded area. "John told me there's a trail back there."

"Do you think we'll get eaten by wolves?" I asked.

He smiled. "It wouldn't be such a bad way to go."

"*What?*" I asked, scrunching up my face at him. "That would be a *horrible* way to go. Can you imagine? That would be terrible."

"I don't know, I thought it would be pretty quick. You know, by the time they all gang up on you, it'd be over in a few seconds."

I gawked at him. "A few of the most devastatingly terrible, horrifying, painful seconds ever!"

He laughed as he stepped toward me. Before I knew what was happening, he was turning me in his arms and positioning me where my back was against his chest. His hand came up right beside my face, and he pointed up the hill. "See that bench over there?" he asked.

I ducked a little, and was able to see it after a few seconds. "Yes," I said.

"The trail ends right there. It's just a lookout. I think we're out of danger of wolves."

He was still standing right behind me, and I got a keen awareness of him all of a sudden—like that feeling a girl gets when she's being touched by a guy—butterflies, as they say.

I stepped out of his grasp and turned to him with a smile, hoping I seemed unaffected. Not wanting to speak for fear of my voice sounding nervous, I held the smile and began walking in the direction of the bench, assuming we'd see a trailhead somewhere.

"There are worse ways to go," he said, as he fell into stride beside me.

"You're right," I said, after giving it a few second's thought.

"I'll bet you saw some unpleasant things growing up in Africa."

"I heard stories, but I didn't have to experience the same types of things those kids live through," I said. I glanced at him with a sad smile and shook my head just a little. "Some of them to endure unspeakable things before they came to the center." I paused, and we walked a few paces in silence. "Wolves would be preferable," I said.

"I'll bet it was hard on you just having to hear stories about what they'd been though," he said. "I can't imagine how it would be growing up around all that."

I glanced at him with a smile as we continued to meander through the mostly-wooded property. "I can't imagine what it would be like to grow up as you," I said as I shrugged. "We're all just who we are. To me, it seems weird to think of *not* growing up in Africa."

"Is that what you want to do when you finish school? Go to Africa like your parents? Raise your family there?"

He glanced at me and I smiled as I shook my head. "I like it in the states," I said. "I'm planning on traveling to Kenya for clinics—probably twice a year, but no, I like living here. I'm not cut out for full-time mission field stuff."

"And you don't think your kids will miss out?"

"Sure they'll miss out," I said. "They'll miss out on growing up in Kenya. But if they lived there, they'd miss out on growing up here."

He chuckled. "So, aside from your regular visits to Kenya, you'll just stay here and work a job as a dentist?"

"A pediatric dentist," I said. "I have a job lined up at a nice place. The plan is to work two or three days a week there and one day at a free clinic in Watts."

"In Watts?" he asked, looking at me like I must be kidding.

I smiled and nodded.

"For real?"

I continued nodding.

"She was serious," he said, referring to London. "You *are* saving the world."

I laughed. "Hardly," I said. "Don't give me too much credit. One day a week in a free clinic is child's play compared to what some people sacrifice for the greater good."

"I try to volunteer about five days a year," he said. "Usually it's a workday at a house that's being built or something like that. My publicist sets it up for me." He glanced at me with a self-deprecating smile. "And here I thought I was so noble for giving freely of my time."

"You are noble," I said. "I shouldn't have said one day a week was child's play. I didn't mean for it to get turned on you or anything. I just meant that compared to what my parents are doing—"

"I know you weren't trying to put it on me," he said, smiling. "I'm the one who did that."

"Not many people even make time to volunteer five times a year," I said.

"So you're saying I *am* noble?"

"I already said you were," I said.

"Maybe I can go to Africa with you sometime," he said. "I'd be nobler if I did that."

"More noble."

He smiled. "I know, but I like nobler. I just wanted to say it. It sort of sounds like cobbler."

"Peach cobbler," I said.

"I'd be the peachiest cobbler if I went to Kenya with you sometime."

That cracked me up for some reason. "The peachiest," I agreed, still laughing.

"Can I really go sometime?" he asked. We were now on the trail leading to the bench, and I glanced at him as we walked. He was looking at me like it was a serious question.

"You mean to my parents' center?"

He nodded.

"Of course you can go there," I said. "They would loooove to have you go there. Are you kidding me?"

"Can I go with *you*?" he asked.

We were walking slowly, and I looked at him with curiosity all over my face. His expression was unreadable. I stared into his eyes as we shuffled slowly along the trail.

He was looking at me the way a man looks at a woman. There was no mistaking it. *Or did he just look at every woman like this? That had to be it. That would explain why every woman on earth was madly in love with him.*

I broke the eye contact, feeling as though I'd just been duped into falling under his spell.

"You can go with me or anyone else," I said. And then, for some regrettable reason, I added, "You can go with London sometime. Her dad's one of my parents' biggest supporters."

"Her dad's amazing," Logan said. "I wish I could have him mentor me through opening a restaurant."

"Why do you want to open a restaurant?" I asked, knowing he didn't need the money.

"I just thought it'd be a good business to have in the family. I'm not a chef or anything. I just like the idea of owning a restaurant—not now, but eventually."

"Well, if anybody could help you be successful with it, he could."

"I know." Logan let out a sigh.

"What?" I asked.

"The problem is, I don't think I'm compatible with London," he said.

I looked at him when he said it, and I tripped when I took my eyes off the path. I didn't fall, but my toe hit against a rock that was planted firmly in the ground, and I jerked forward, almost tumbling, but catching myself with a jerking motion instead. Thank goodness we were walking slowly. It could have been a lot worse. Logan reached out and caught me by the shoulders, helping me to regain my balance. I didn't even have time to think about how embarrassed I was about tripping, because I was too distracted by the feel of his hands on my shoulders. I shrugged out of his grasp, feeling overwhelmed by my physical reaction to his touch.

"You okay?" he asked.

I laughed as I looked back and pointed to the rock I had tripped over. "I tripped in front of you just now, and I don't even care, because I thought I heard you say *you don't think you and London are compatible.*"

"I don't think we are," he said.

I let out a long, sigh, letting my shoulders sag, and squinting my eyes, showing my distress.

"I didn't think that would come as a shock to you," he said.

I looked at him curiously, and he continued, "Don't tell me you two are as close as she says you are. I can tell already that you're nothing alike."

I slowly began walking again, but this time I kept my eyes on the path. "What if I said you're totally off base and we're thick as thieves?" I asked.

"You wouldn't say that," he said.

"How do you know?"

"Because you'd be lying, and you don't lie—or at least, you're terrible at it."

My eyes widened. "How do you know that?" I asked. "Are you some sort of mind reader or something?"

He smiled wryly at me. "Aw, come on, you don't believe in that either."

I laughed.

"So why are you disappointed to hear me say I don't like her?" he asked.

"Because if you break up with her, I'm gonna be stuck with the heartbroken version of her for the next few days..." I hesitated. "And honestly, I can't imagine that."

"That'd be some Kenya-style stuff right there," he said, laughing.

"Kenya ain't got nothin' on mad London," I said.

We both laughed at the thought.

"She's not my girlfriend," he said. "I wouldn't be breaking up with her."

"I think she'd see it differently," I said.

He sighed as he absentmindedly reached out to snap the end of a limb off a nearby tree. "We're not together," he said. "That's all I know. I met her back east a few months ago, and we've been talking a little. I guess I hoped I'd grow to like her or whatever, but I don't think it's gonna work out."

"Why'd you want to grow to like her?" I asked.

He didn't answer right away.

"Her dad?" I asked, as soon as the thought occurred to me.

He remained quiet. "It sounds bad, I know," he said, finally.

"I think she's used to getting special treatment because of her dad," I said. "She may not even mind if you're just dating for that."

"I'm not dating her," he said. "That's what I'm telling you."

"But you're trying to stop talking to her?" I asked, dreading the backlash of what he was getting at.

He laughed. "There's nothing to break off. I told you, we're not together."

I let out a defeated huff as we walked, which made him chuckle at me. "You're funny," he said.

"Why?"

"Because you're acting disappointed that I'm not interested in a girl you probably don't even like. I'm not sure how I feel about that."

"What do you mean?"

He smiled. "I wanted you to say something like, *'Yeah Logan, she totally stinks. I think talking to her is a terrible idea. I think you should get my number instead'*."

I just stopped right in the middle of the path and stared at him, unable to believe the words that were coming from his mouth. What was even funnier was that he said the whole phrase in a high-pitched, girly voice, doing a bad imitation of me.

"Well, I can't say that," I said.

"Why not?" he asked.

I stared at him for a few seconds. "I would never say that," I said. "Because I'd be the one dealing with the heartbreak, remember? She's staying at *my* house."

"You couldn't care less that I just told you I'm interested in getting your number," he said as more of a statement than a question.

We weren't far from the bench, but we stopped in the middle of the path and just stood there, staring at each other. "If I thought you were serious about wanting my number, which I don't, I would tell you that it was a terrible idea." I smiled. "I would add that I'm flattered because you're handsome, and charming, and I really like your movies, but I'd tell you it would never work."

"You know saying that just makes me want to try to make it work, right?"

I laughed. "I'm sure there are plenty of other girls out there who'll do a convincing job of pretending to be aloof if that's what does it for you," I said.

"London's already doing that," he said. "How do you think I get by with no commitment?"

We stared at each other for a few long seconds before I gave him a regretful smile. "You're funny," I said.

He narrowed his eyes at me slightly and gave me a little smirk. "I'm not trying to make you laugh."

Chapter 5

I smiled and shook my head at Logan as I took the last few steps to the bench. It was a concrete bench with no backrest that was long enough for three people to sit comfortably. I sat on one end and he sat on the other, leaving a foot or so of space between us. We looked out at the gorgeous view of Santa Barbara and the ocean. My eyes fell onto the movie set commotion just below us before I glanced at Logan. He saw me look at him from the corner of his eye and turned my way.

"I wasn't trying to be funny," he repeated with a smirk. It had been so long since we last spoke that I had nearly forgotten why he was saying that.

Did this guy really expect me to believe he was interested in me? Was that what he was saying?

"Well, you're not serious, I can tell you that."

"Why would you say that?" he asked.

I let out a laugh, not knowing how to handle this conversation. He just stared at me as if waiting to hear my answer.

"I'm confused," I said, finally.

"About what?"

"About what you're saying," I said.

"What's confusing about it?"

"Did you just ask me for my phone number?" I asked, not knowing how else to put it. I giggled as the words left my mouth. It seemed so wrong. I was just waiting to hear him laugh like I had misunderstood.

He did laugh. "Yes, I asked you for your number. Or maybe I said I wanted you to ask for mine. Either way, the idea was that I'd be able to reach you once London goes back home."

I giggled again. "See?"

He shook his head, confused. "See what?"

"You. You can't just say that we should call each other when London leaves. That's just weird."

"Why's it weird?"

"Well, for one, I'm pretty sure she thinks she's your girlfriend, and I don't really want her to find out that we had this conversation."

"What else?" he asked.

"You just met me," I said. "We don't even know each other."

"That's the whole point. I'm trying to get to know you."

I laughed.

"What?"

"You," I said.

"What about me?"

"You must be used to getting any girl you want."

"I'm not trying to get girls," he said. "I work, and I chill with my family and friends. You're acting like I walk around saying this stuff to every girl I meet."

"It would seem that way since you're so well-versed at it."

He laughed. "If I was so well-versed, you'd be giving me your number right now instead of giving me a hard time. Come on, I don't want to put it off. I don't know what's gonna happen with London, and I don't know how else to reach you."

"It's better if you don't reach me," I said. Before he could say anything, I added, "And I know that just makes it seem like more of a challenge or whatever, but please don't think of it that way." I smiled at him. "I don't mean any disrespect at all. I'm a fan of your movies. I'm actually a little star struck to meet you. But nothing could ever come of this." I gestured back and forth between us. "We're too different."

He flinched. "How do you know that?"

"Because, I just do."

"That's not good enough."

I scrunched up my face at him, wondering why in the world we were having this conversation.

"Name a reason," he said.

"Because I'm a missionary's kid, and you're… well, you're *you*."

"That's not good enough at all," he said. "That barely even made sense."

"Because you're with London."

"I'm not with her," he said. "Not even close." He smiled at me—that devastatingly charming smile. "What else?"

"You and I expect different things out of a relationship, and it's best not to even entertain the idea of one when that's the case."

He gave me an amused grin. "Why's it such an ordeal to get your phone number?"

"Because the only reason you want it is because it's such an ordeal!"

He laughed. "That's not true."

I groaned at the thought of coming right out and saying it, but it had to be said. It was the only thing that could end this ridiculous conversation.

"I'm a virgin," I said, feeling waves of anxious nerves course through my body the instant the word left my lips.

He was silent, looking out at the ocean, and I smiled at the serious look on his face. "Also, I plan on remaining that way," I added.

Logan continued to stare as if really taking in what I was saying.

I reached out and pushed at his leg, letting out a little laugh. "I didn't mean to get all heavy on you or anything. It's not usually one of the first things on the list to say about myself. It just seemed like the most logical thing to say to make you understand where I was coming from. I knew it'd be an issue." I paused and stared at his profile while he remained quiet for a few more seconds.

"How old are you?" he asked.

"Twenty-five."

He turned to face me, staring straight into my eyes. His were dark brown around the edges with lighter, golden brown near the inside. "And you've seriously never..."

"Never," I said. I smiled past my blushing cheeks. "I know it probably makes you see me differently, but trust me, it's better to get it out of the way before we waste either of our time." I laughed, hoping to move on to less embarrassing topics. "Not to mention, I'm slightly scared of London."

Again, we were quiet for a few long heartbeats.

"And you thought you'd just tell me that, and I'd leave you alone?"

"Yes."

"Hmm."

Another minute of silence passed between us. I wondered what he was thinking or if he'd ever talk again. "You're saving yourself for marriage?" he asked, finally.

I smiled. "I know it makes me sound like a big dork. Like I said, it's not something I go around telling people when we first meet or anything."

He pulled back and stared at me, taking me in from head to foot. "I just can't believe you're twenty-five and you're untouched," he said. "That makes me catch all sorts of feelings about you."

I laughed and shook my head. "I thought you'd run for the hills, but part of me isn't surprised you'd see it as a challenge."

"Why can't you assume I'd fall somewhere in the middle?"

I shrugged.

"Can't we just forget you ever said that, and say, *'hi, I'm Logan'* and *'hi, I'm Rachel'* again?"

"Not really," I said.

"Why not?"

"Because that's the whole point. If we went out, we'd have two very different ideas of how the evening would end."

"That's assuming I'd try to sleep with you on the first date."

"Or the second, or third, or fifth." I smiled at him and pushed at his leg again. "Let's talk about something else," I said. "I'm feeling all shy now."

"Like what?"

"How about sports?" I asked, absentmindedly kicking my feet as they hung from the bench.

"Sports?" he asked. "What do you know about sports?"

"I'm a baseball fan. I try to see at least a few Dodgers games every year. I like basketball, too."

"Is that where you want me to take you?" he asked. "A Dodgers game? I can get us some box seats… or courtside for the Lakers."

I laughed, "I'll bet you could."

"So, it's a date."

"It's not a date," I said, shaking my head at him playfully. "And the whole point of talking about sports was to not talk about dates, remember?"

"I can't help it," he said, smiling innocently. "Our conversation just keeps going back to that."

I narrowed my eyes at him, which made him laugh.

We talked about baseball and basketball, which led to a conversation about music. Then we talked about a ton of random things we thought were funny. We laughed, and talked, and thank goodness, he never brought up exchanging numbers again. Several times, different groups would come up the hillside lookout, but no one ever came close enough to make us discontinue our conversation.

We'd been sitting there for an hour or two when Logan leaned over to dig his phone out of his pocket. "Your friend's blowing up my phone," he said, looking down at it.

I dug mine out of the small bag that was sitting on the bench next to me. "She's blowing up mine, too."

"I can't believe they're on their way back already," he said, scrolling through the messages. "It seems like they just left."

"They are?" I asked, looking at my phone. "I don't think I have a message saying that."

"It was the one she just sent."

"Crazy that we've been up here long enough for them to make it to L.A.," I said, stashing my phone back into my bag.

"I hate it that she's coming back," he said.

I laughed. "Is it bad to admit that I was just feeling the same way?"

"I knew you were into me," he said.

"I'm really not," I said. I did my best to sound convincing even though it was a *blatant lie*. The more I talked to him, the more I liked him. I needed to stop the situation before I got into trouble, but that was easier said than done.

He stood right in front of me and I looked up at him from my position on the bench. We had each gotten up a time or two to stretch during our chat, but this time, it seemed like he was standing to walk back down the hill. I got up to walk with him, but he didn't move. He just stared at me with a tiny smirk playing at the corner of his mouth.

"You're not?" he asked, referring to my proclamation that I wasn't into him.

"No," I said.

I smiled and broke eye contact with him as I said it.

"You're the worst liar in the whole world," he said, with a laugh. "You'd be a terrible actress."

"Thank goodness for dental school," I said. "And, to answer your question, I wasn't saying I don't want London to come back because of *you*. I was just saying it because I don't really feel like hanging out with her."

He smiled. "And you're a little jealous."

"No," I said. "You don't even like her, so even if I *was* going to be jealous over you, which I'm not, it wouldn't be because of her."

"I'd be jealous over you," he said, causing my stomach to flip. "If you had some guy texting you all the time and telling everybody he was you're boyfriend, I'd be jealous."

"I do have that," I said.

His expression was comically confused like he couldn't believe what I was saying.

"It's really not a big deal," I said smiling at his unexpected reaction. "We've just been out a few times, it's not serious or anything."

"I thought you said you don't date guys just to date them."

"I don't. Not when I don't feel like it could eventually lead to marriage."

"Oh, so now you're *marrying* this guy? We've been talking for two hours, and you never mention having a boyfriend, but now I find out you're practically *married*."

I giggled. "I'm far from married."

"But you *could* marry him?"

I shrugged and nodded. "I guess. I mean, there's at least potential."

"And there's not with me."

I smiled at him, but he just stared at me like he wanted me to answer his non-question.

"We were having so much fun," I said, pushing at his shoulder.

"So, let's not stop," he said. He pulled me into his arms, and I was helpless to resist. He held me securely around the shoulders, and I gently wrapped my arms around his waist. I knew better, yet I could do nothing to stop myself. I was comfortable with hugs. I'd grown up in a hugging family, so I blamed my instinct to hug him on that.

"I'm definitely jealous of this guy, whoever he is," Logan said.

And just like that, the spell was broken. Whatever trance I'd been in came crashing to a halt at Logan's mention of Ashton.

I let go of him and stepped back, causing him to let out a sigh. He reached out with a playful pinch to my arm. "That was good," he said. "Why'd you have to go way over there?"

"Because," I said. "You make me feel crazy. You make me do crazy stuff."

"You make me feel crazy, too," he said. "That makes two of us." He hesitated for a few seconds before adding, "Can I show you something?"

I sort of nodded and smiled as I asked, "What?"

He licked his lips. I was so distracted by it that I hardly noticed when he stepped toward me. In one quick motion, he came closer and ducked to put his lips right on mine. It was so quick and gentle that I lost my senses and went along with it. It was as if I was standing outside of my own body. Before I knew what I was doing, I tilted my head up, leaning into him. A warm wave of desire washed over me as

I drank in the feel of his lips on me. They were soft and warm, and they conformed perfectly to mine. I let out a quiet whimper at the gut wrenching feeling of longing, and then pulled back to look at him. I felt like I could melt into a big gooey puddle right down on the ground.

"Logan," I whispered. I pointed at his chest and narrowed my eyes playfully him. "You're gonna be in trouble if you keep trying to get *me* in trouble."

"I'm the one who's in trouble here, Rachel. I'm just trying to go to work and have a normal day, and you've got me up here having all these feelings. I feel like I want to go have a little talk with that other guy right now—tell him you're mine."

"Ashton?" I asked, not sure what he was talking about.

"Is that dude's name, Ashton?" he asked.

I nodded.

"Like Kutcher?"

I nodded. "It *is* Ashton Kutcher," I said.

Logan looked at me sideways. "It is?"

I nodded again.

"Seriously?"

I continued nodding with a straight face.

"You think Ashton Kutcher's gonna be good *husband material*?" he asked.

I cracked up laughing. "I'm just messin' with you. His name really is Ashton, though." I raised my eyebrows at him. "Guess I'm a pretty good actress after all,"

He laughed. "You're terrible, I'm just too messed up to see it. I was tripping, thinking you'd date some other actor but not me."

I couldn't help but laugh at his reaction. I'd been laughing for the last two hours. My cheeks were sore.

"Tell me you didn't feel anything just now," he said, touching my arm. I knew what he was referring to, and I hesitated, wondering how to respond.

"I can't tell you that."

"See?"

"That doesn't mean anything," I said.

"It means everything. Do you feel like that with that other guy?"

"Do you feel like that with all the other girls?"

"No, I don't. That's exactly what I'm saying."

Chapter 6

It seemed like London was gone for two seconds. It had taken them nearly four hours, and it felt as if they had just left when I saw them walking toward us.

Logan and I had been together the whole time they were gone. We spent some time up on the hillside before heading to his trailer where we hung out with his friends Phillip and Nico. It was fairly small, so we were right up in each other's faces, but I liked them; we had fun together. Their personalities were similar to Logan's. I could see why they were all best friends. We were in there together for about an hour, and they all treated me like they knew me their whole lives.

Logan and I had gone back outside and were sitting at one of the picnic tables when London and Kai returned. We could see them from far off, and Logan started talking out of the side of his mouth the instant we noticed them.

"You know I'm gonna have to get your number, right?" he asked stiffly and quietly.

Kai headed in one direction, and London, who had noticed us by then, headed straight for us.

"We've already talked about this." I said, without moving my lips at all.

He looked at me, but I continued looking at London, who was smiling as she approached.

"Please forget about that other guy," he said, looking straight at the side of my face as I continued to smile at London.

"How about your girlfriend who's walking up to us right now?" I asked, still smiling stiffly.

"I'm telling her something right now," he said, as if he had to prove something to me.

My head whipped around, and I regarded him with a pleading expression. I didn't even care that he and I were staring straight at each other while she was fast approaching.

"Please don't," I whispered.

"Then stop calling her that," he said.

"Heyyyy!" London said, coming to sit next to Logan at the picnic table. We had been sitting on the same side of the table, so now there were three of us on that one bench. "I had no idea we were going to Los Angeles just now!" she said, beaming at him. "That was insane!"

She leaned over Logan to look at me. "I'm so sorry I left you for so long," she said.

"No problem," I said. "It seemed like it went really fast."

"I'm glad it did for you," she said. She tried to look annoyed, but she couldn't contain a smile. Her attention shifted back to Logan, and she started wiggling and jiggling in her seat. She shook her fists and let out a little squeal. "And guess what?" she said, excitedly.

"What?" he asked, less than interested.

"I get to be in the movie with you!" Her voice was about three octaves too high. I knew she had been trying to play it cool around Logan, but this was just too much for her to handle. She was jigging all around. "Can you believe it? I get to be in a movie! My big Hollywood debut! Well, Kai said he'd talk to the director for me. But I think he'll say yes. Kai seemed to think he would. Kai's a doll. We got along like two peas in a pod. Thank you for talking to Rachel. I didn't mean to leave her here for so long. I hope she wasn't in anybody's way."

Logan turned away from her and looked at me with a wide-eyed *please rescue me* expression.

"I stayed out of everybody's way," I said. "In fact, most of the time, I was way up there on the hillside. There's a bench up there, and I sat on it, totally alone. With no one else. Just me... alone on the bench."

I couldn't resist teasing Logan. The more I said, the bigger his eyes got. Technically, it wasn't lying if I was being weird enough for the person to know something was up.

"Completely alone." I added, dramatically and with a silly accent.

Logan tried, but couldn't contain a laugh. It was obvious by the way it burst from his mouth that he'd been trying to hold it in, but failed.

"Y'all are being crazy," London said, looking back and forth between Logan and me.

He gestured to the hillside. "She's lying," he said. "Truth is, I went up there with her, and we made out the whole time."

I let out an accidental laugh that I disguised as a cough. London started laughing as if that would *never* happen.

Logan stood before turning to face us. "I need to go, ladies," he said. He looked at me, and pointed straight at me. "You're in trouble," he said, with only the slightest hint of a smile.

"What happened?" London asked, like she thought I'd made some kind of dumb mistake on set or something.

"She knows," he said, still looking at me. My eyes widened slightly as I begged him without words to please, for the love of all that is good in the world, *not* say anymore. He smiled right at me, enjoying watching me squirm.

"What do you know, Rachel," she said as he turned to walk away. "What did you do?"

Her tone was rude, which made Logan turn around. "She didn't do anything wrong," he clarified. "We've been cutting up. It's just an inside joke we have."

He turned and continued walking, leaving me with one very curious London sitting next to me. "Did he just say you have an *inside joke*?" she asked, looking annoyed.

"I think so," I said.

"What's the joke?" she said.

"I don't even remember," I said. It was true; I didn't remember what he had said. Oh yeah, I think he said I was in trouble.

"He's just being silly," I said.

"Silly?" There was all sorts of flair in the way she said the word. Obviously, she didn't like the familiarity it implied.

"He couldn't work till you came back," I said. "We hung out. He's a nice guy."

"You hung out with my boyfriend?" she asked. Her emphasis was on the words *hung out*, as if they implied too much as well.

I wanted so badly to say that he wasn't her boyfriend, but I held the words in my mouth. They fought and fought, and almost came out, but I somehow managed to hold them in.

"What's your problem?" she asked.

"I don't have a problem," I said. "I had a good day." I wanted to add, "*Until you just got here*," but I didn't. "Don't you have to get ready for your big scene?" I asked, instead, wanting to be left alone.

"I'm not doing it today. Kai said it'll probably be tomorrow or Monday."

***

It was never the same with Logan after London got back from her trip to L.A. She didn't let me out of her sight for the remainder of the weekend. I had hoped she'd get to walk on as an extra so that she would leave me alone, but Kai couldn't pull the necessary strings to get her a job, so I was stuck with her.

Once the director had everything he needed to get started, Logan became extremely busy. London and I hung out 'on set' but couldn't really get close enough to see much. Logan made a little time to hang out with us, but I knew he wasn't looking forward to spending time with her.

It was Monday morning when it all came crashing down. She sashayed onto the property wearing a wide-brimmed hat and oversized sunglasses. Logan was standing with a small group of people including one of his co-stars. He left them and walked toward us. There seemed to be purpose in his approach. He was already dressed for whatever scene they were about to film, and I couldn't help but notice how sharp he looked.

My heart skipped a beat, but maybe that was more about the fact that he wouldn't take his eyes off me. I was walking right next to London, and he didn't even acknowledge that she was there.

"I need to talk to you for just a second," he said, lifting his chin at me slightly. He turned to look at London for the first time. "I need to talk to Rachel for a second," he said to her. "You can wait here. We'll be right back."

Her expression reflected her displeasure.

"Okay, so we'll be back in a second." Logan turned me by the shoulder and we walked ten or twelve paces before coming to the edge of one of the tents where we could have partial privacy.

"What in the world, Logan?" I asked.

"I can't take it anymore," he said. "I have to set London straight. She can't go on thinking we're talking or whatever. I don't even care for her as a person, much less want to date her."

"Can't you just wait till she goes back home?" I asked, already dreading the backlash.

"Please tell me how to reach you, Rachel. The only reason I haven't told her anything sooner is because I wanted you around." He reached out and touched my arm, and it sent a shock wave running up my spine. I hadn't made physical contact with him in two days, and I had forgotten the effects of it.

"Logan, I like you, but we can't," I whispered.

"Why not?"

"Because of everything I told you two days ago."

"That's ridiculous," he said.

"That I'm waiting for marriage?" I asked.

"No, it's ridiculous that you felt the need to bring it up. Like you think it's was all I'm interested in."

I looked at him with a smile, and he regarded me with an expression that seemed sincere. "Give me anything," he said. "Please. Tell me how to reach you. I'm telling her goodbye, and I don't want the same for you."

I stared at him, not even caring that London could see us from where she was standing.

"Let me prove it," he said.

"Prove what?"

"Prove that I'd wait for you."

"How?"

"I don't know. Test me."

I risked a glance at London to find that she was glaring at us. I sighed as I met his eyes again.

"Give me your number," I said. "I'll call you in a year."

"*A year?*" he asked.

"A year."

"Why so long?"

"Because you'll get tired of waiting and move on by then," is said. "You won't even remember me a year from now."

"That's not true, but I'll do it if it makes you take my number." He held out his hand and moved his fingers letting me know he wanted me to hand him something. "Give me your phone," he said. "If you don't call my number by next September, I'll be forced to have Nico look you up."

"You won't care by then," I said, confidently, handing him my phone.

"Do you *want* me to forget?" he asked as he tapped out his number on the screen.

I didn't answer him.

I would be lying if I said yes.

He looked me in the eyes. "You can test me all you want," he said. "I want you to. I'm not giving up."

I smiled as put I my phone back into my purse.

"September," he said.

I felt like I wanted to throw myself into his arms and say why wait, let's just be together right now this very second, but I couldn't. I had to give him something, though. I had to let him know that the feelings were mutual.

"The bench was my favorite part," I said. I smiled at him and watched as his smile faded.

He looked straight at my mouth. I knew what he was thinking. "Don't you even think about it," I said.

He grinned at me, and I smiled back.

"I'm gonna do it," he said.

"Don't you dare," I said.

"Just so you know, I can do a year standing on my head," he said, challengingly.

"Oh, you can?"

"Yes."

"And what happens after that?" I asked.

"Well, obviously you're mine after that."

My smile broadened. "Oh, is that how it works?"

"Yep."

I knew he'd give up and move on without me, which was better for both of us, but it was fun to fantasize that he would actually tough it out. I could just image reconnecting. In those few seconds, I romanticized a whole reunion scene in my head.

"You know you have to go without sex for that year, right?" I asked, just making sure we both knew the terms.

"That's the whole point," he said nodding.

"And then after that year, I'm still not gonna sleep with anyone until I get married."

He nodded as if the terms were obvious. "You know you have to break up with that Ashton Kutcher dude, right?"

I laughed. "I can do a year standing on my head," I said, repeating his phrase.

"Great, so can I," he said.

London must have been fed up with waiting because the next thing I knew, she was standing right beside us.

"What can you do?" London asked.

"A year standing on my head," Logan replied.

"A year of what?" she asked.

"Of anything." He looked at me. "I think we were just finishing up, right?"

I gave him a curt nod. "Right."

He looked at London. "We're shooting inside today, and then wrapping up after that. I'll be headed back home tonight." He said it with the finality of someone who was saying goodbye.

"Do you want us to leave?" she asked.

He nodded. "You wouldn't get to see anything today anyway." He paused and seemed as if he was considering something. "Hey," he added. "I'm not sure if I'll be able to see you again on your trip."

"Oh really?"

"Yeah. Actually, can I talk to you for a second?"

Chapter 7

Logan probably broke it to London as tactfully as he could, but she didn't take it well. She gave some serious consideration to catching the next flight home, but decided to stay in L.A. and shop away her sorrows. She never told me what Logan said to her that day, but I assumed it was that he couldn't see or talk to her anymore.

I wondered if she would ask me what he said to me when we talked, (especially since she saw me hand him my telephone) but she didn't—it was like she was trying not to notice it happened. She never mentioned it, but that didn't mean it got past her. She knew something had transpired between us, and she took it out on me in her passive-aggressive way for the rest of her trip. She was flat out catty, which did nothing but make me feel sad for her.

Thankfully, the remaining days went quickly, and before I knew it, London was on a plane, headed back to South Carolina. I thought about Logan a lot for the first few weeks. I'd scroll past his name in my contacts, letting my finger hover over the button as I contemplated reaching out to him. I watched a few of his movies and searched him on the internet, but every time I did that, it made me want to call him— if for nothing else, than to prove to myself that his number worked, or that I hadn't dreamed the whole thing.

As bad as the temptation was, I didn't do it. I meant what I said when I told him I didn't mess around with relationships that could get me in trouble, and I figured that sticking to the plan of waiting a year was the most logical way to put our connection to the test. I didn't have my heart set on him waiting for me, but if he didn't, it wouldn't have worked out anyway.

But what if he waits? What if I contact him in September, and he tells me there's no one else? What then? I remembered back to the conversation we had and thought he said something like 'I'd be his'. I wondered what it'd be like to be *his*? I thought it might not be so bad.

I made lots of deals with God during those months. Well, mostly just one deal, it just got reworded and rethought several times as the weeks and months passed. Basically, I asked God to please let Logan move on if he wasn't meant for me. I sort of had it in my head that if Logan was still interested when September rolled around, that would be my sign that he was the one, and I could and should jump into a relationship with him feet first.

I broke things off with Ashton. It was probably naïve of me to do that when Logan was, in all likelihood, seeing other women, but somewhere in my heart, I felt spoken-for.

The waiting was hard—especially at first, but school kept me busy. I finished in May and had plans to take a couple of months off before starting my practice. I'd worked my butt off for the past eight years, and I needed a second to stop and catch my breath. The plan was to spend all of June relaxing at the beach like I had nothing better to do, and then go to Kenya for two weeks before starting work.

I was still in the beginning of my *relax at the beach* phase and was loving every second of it. I had been sitting in a lawn chair all afternoon with my toes in the sand, and I didn't feel guilty about it at all. I didn't feel guilty about the delicious, super-fresh sushi that I was about to eat, either.

I saw Kate, Victor, and Charles waiting for me at the sushi bar as soon as I walked in the door. They were all good friends of mine from dental school. We had grown so close during our training that we made a promise to get together regularly afterward, and this was our first date since graduation. They all greeted me as "Dr. Stephens" when I sat down, which made us all laugh.

"This place is fa-a-ancy," I said, being silly as I took a seat on the end next to Victor.

"Is this your first time here?" Victor asked.

I nodded as I looked around. Most sushi places I'd gone to had some sort of cheap looking things scattered about, like the brightly colored ceramic cat with one paw up in the air, or a poorly framed poster of all the types of sushi they offered. Not this one. It was upscale with a capital U. There was nothing cheap about it. Even the barstool was heavy as I scooted toward the counter on it.

"First time, yes," I said, remembering that Victor had just asked me a question.

"Charles has had these reservations for weeks, by the way," Kate said, leaning forward to talk to me over the bar.

"We had to have reservations for the *bar*?" I asked.

"You have to have reservations to even say the *name* Sakura," Charles said.

"What's so special about it?" I asked.

"The chef's an artist. You don't tell him what you want, he just makes you a plate of food, and you eat it."

"What happens if you don't like it?" I asked.

"That won't happen," Victor said, confidently.

"I think you guys told me about this place," I said.

"It's really popular. They're only open three nights a week, and they only feed fifty people a night. It's a supply and demand thing. People kill for reservations."

Sure, it was the summer of celebration, but old habits die hard, and I hated to waste money on what I considered overly-lavish things. "How much does something like this cost?" I asked, tactfully in Victor's ear.

Victor used his thumb to gesture to Charles, who was sitting at the far end on the other side of Kate. "Charles wanted to do this as a graduation present," Victor said. He leaned closer to me. "But if you wanted to know for the future, it's two hundred dollars a person."

"Thank you for this," I said, leaning forward to address Charles. He smiled and winked at me. "You're very welcome. You earned it."

"You did too," I said with a smile. "Maybe I'll buy you some ice cream after this."

He reached out to give me a fist bump.

"Oh my goodness, oh my goodness, oh my goodness," Kate whispered.

She had turned around to adjust her purse strap, but she was now stunned and wide-eyed, staring straight at the rows of fish lined up in front of us at the sushi bar. We all just looked at her like she was crazy.

"Don't look now," she whispered slowly. "Don't even look close to now. Wait like thirty seconds, and when you *do* look, don't do it all at the same time."

"What is wrong with you?" Charles asked.

Victor immediately swiveled in his stool and started scanning the room to try to see what she was talking about.

"What is it?" I asked him.

I was trying to play it cool and keep my eyes on Kate, but it was hard—especially seeing how shaken up she was.

"I don't see anything," Victor said. "It's just people sitting at tables, eating fish."

"If I'm looking at twelve o'clock right now," she whispered, still staring straight ahead at the fish, "then he's at seven or eight o'clock. Don't look now."

"Behind us?" asked Victor, turning instantly.

"Don't stare," Kate whispered frantically.

"I don't even see anything," Victor said.

He looked in that direction for several seconds, but turned with a shrug once he didn't see what she was talking about.

"Still just people eating fish," he said.

Charles was the next to turn. "Ohh," he said with a knowing smile. "It's that guy from *Killing Streak*." He smiled at Kate. "Is that who you were talking about?"

She nodded stiffly, which I barely even noticed because my gut was tied in knots at the mere mention of that movie. It was one Logan had starred in. Of course, there were other actors in it as well. I told myself that it was one of the other ones she'd seen.

"Are you talking about Logan Ritchie?" Victor asked, turning again.

"Uh, huh," Kate said, nodding dazedly. "I'm really nervous," she said, leaning past Victor to speak to me. "I heard some stars come in here, but I've never seen one. Can you believe it?"

"You sure it's him?" Victor asked after looking again.

"Definitely." She looked at me and nudged her head in in Logan's general direction. "Look," she said. "You know what he looks like, don't you?"

I nodded, but I had trouble swallowing past the lump in my throat.

"What's wrong?" she asked.

"Nothing," I said, managing a smile.

"Look behind you and tell me that's not Logan Ritchie sitting over there," she said.

"I don't think it's him," Victor said. "I don't think he'd be caught dead wearing those goofball glasses."

"Movie stars don't care about wearing crazy stuff like that," Kate said. "They do it on purpose so people won't think it's them. Obviously, his date doesn't think they're too goofy looking."

"He does have a hot girlfriend," Charles said.

"It's totally him," Kate whispered, taking a sip of her tea. "Is it okay for me to ask him for his autograph?"

Forget doing flips or being tied in knots, my stomach was roaring like an angry ocean during a storm. I honestly felt that fight or flight reflex that had me wanting to run for the door. For some strange reason, I had myself convinced that September would roll around and I would ride off into the sunset with that guy, and the thought of him eating good sushi with a gorgeous blonde made me more upset than I cared to admit.

How did I know he was with a gorgeous blonde, you ask. Because I turned and looked at them the second Charles said he had a hot girlfriend.

It was Logan. There was no doubt in my mind. I stared at him for several long seconds before turning my attention to his beautiful, fashionably dressed companion.

"Those are some goofy glasses, though," Kate said, after stealing one more glance. "Do you think I could go ask him for an autograph?"

I had a ton of thoughts all at once. Part of me wanted to march right over there with her just so Logan would know that I saw them together and that all bets were off. *He probably hadn't even been betting with me in the first place.* I had several more cynical thoughts like that before finally deciding to come out with the truth to my friends.

"I sort of know him," I said.

"You do?" Kate asked.

"What'd she say?" Charles asked.

"She said she knows him."

"Logan Ritchie?" he asked, looking at me as if he must be mistaken.

"How?" Victor asked.

"It's a long story," I said. "It was from when that girl London was staying at my house."

Kate laughed, obviously remembering some of the stories I told her. I had conveniently left out the part where I met, and maybe fell in love with Logan.

I figured it wasn't big news since most women in America were also in love with him.

"Take me over there," she pleaded.

Just then our server came by to bring a fresh pot of green tea and give us an update on our meal. We spoke with him for a second, but it was hard for me to pay attention with the chaos that was happening in my own heart.

This whole time, I'd been telling myself nothing would ever come of everything that happened last September, but I must have still had my heart set on it, because seeing him with her wasn't fun for me. I hated the idea of him being there with someone else. Part of me wanted to confront him, and the other part wanted to make an effort not to let him see me at all.

"Would he remember you if you went over there?" Kate asked.

I nodded. "I think so," I said.

I felt like I was in some alternate reality. It was a delirious feeling that I attributed to the nervous energy coursing through my body.

"Please can we?" she asked. "I'd really like to meet him."

"I don't think we should interrupt their date, "I said.

"I'm sure he's used to it," Victor countered.

"I don't think I want to do that," I said, reluctantly.

87

"The restroom's that way," Kate said. "We could just walk by there on our way to the restroom. If he happens to remember you, fine. If not, we won't bother them."

A crippling wave of nerves hit me at the thought. My knees started tingling, and I felt that even if I did decide to go over there, I wouldn't be able to walk right.

"Come on, let's go before the sushi gets here," she urged.

"No," I said, shaking my head.

"Please!" she begged. "It's probably the only time I'll ever get to meet someone that famous."

"I'm too nervous," I said.

"Why? You said you've already met him. And besides, all we're doing is going to the restroom. No pressure."

I was quiet for a few seconds before I narrowed my eyes at her as if to say *you'll owe me for this.* "I'm not walking right by his table," I said.

"Fine," she replied, already standing. "Let's go."

Chapter 8

Everything seemed so surreal as I got to my feet with the intention of heading to the restroom with Kate. The adrenaline made it feel like cold waves of air were hitting my body. The hallway leading to the restroom was on the other side of the small dining room. We didn't have to walk directly next to Logan's table to get there, but we had to go in that general direction. I had planned on not looking at all, but it was literally impossible to keep myself from glancing at his table.

He was smiling and chatting it up with the lovely blonde, which caused an ache in my chest. I was still staring at him when he caught our movement out of the corner of his eye and glanced our way. Having been caught staring took me by surprise, and I broke eye contact instantly, smiling casually as I did.

"This is a nice place," I said to Kate as we walked.

It was the stupidest thing ever to say, but I felt like I might burst into a thousand pieces from all the nerves. She gave me a courtesy giggle, but she was just about as nervous as I was and didn't really care what I was saying anyway.

I led the way, and we walked quickly down the short hallway into the ladies room.

"Oh my goodness, oh my goodness, oh my goodness, that was him for sure!" she said as the door closed behind us.

There was only one stall in the restroom, and its door was wide open, so I knew we were alone. I took a deep, calming breath and leaned against the wall.

"He looked straight at you!" she said. "Did you see that?"

I nodded, still taking deep breaths.

"I think he recognized you!"

I paced a little, trying to calm my racing heart. "We have to play it cool," I said. "When we go back out there, we shouldn't look that way at all—just go straight to our seats. Don't even glance."

"I can't stop from looking," she said. "It doesn't matter. I'm sure he's used to it."

I had seen movies where someone was in the restroom at a public place and they snuck out of the window to avoid whatever the other option was. That sort of escape felt like a reasonable idea at this point, and if the restroom would have had a window, I honestly might have used it. The only alternative was an air duct, but that was even sillier than going through a window.

"Do you need to pee?" Kate asked.

I shook my head.

"Me neither. I guess we could wash our hands."

I stared at my hands absentmindedly as I scrubbed and rinsed.

"I'm excited about the sushi," she said.

I smiled and nodded, but was completely preoccupied with what... *who* was on the other side of that door.

"Just talk to me the whole way back to our seats so that we look busy," I whispered as we opened the door.

No sooner did the last word leave my lips did I see Logan standing in the hallway. He was just standing there, leaning against the wall, waiting. Our eyes met for a split second before I quickly glanced at the wall behind him. I realized as soon as I looked away that I had to look back at him. He was smiling at me. I couldn't just ignore him. I was so nervous that I had to *make* myself focus on him again. All this was taking place while Kate and I were walking out of the bathroom, and it caused an awkward few seconds in the hall where we weren't sure whether to walk or stand still.

Finally, I just stood up straight and looked Logan in the eyes with a smile. He had taken off the glasses, and his eyes seemed bottomless in the dimly lit hallway. I felt a bit like my body was on the verge of melting. He had on dark fitted jeans and a T-shirt with a baby-blue windbreaker. He was smiling straight at me.

"Rachel?" he asked.

"Hey!" I said.

He pumped his fist excitedly the way hot, confident guys do. "I knew it!" he said, as if his team had just scored some points. "What are you doing here?"

Another lady came to the restroom, and Kate and I moved aside to let her pass. She stared at Logan the whole time, and I knew her trip to the restroom had been more about seeing him than going in there. I experienced a stab of jealousy at the way she looked at him, which was ludicrous since he had a *real date* sitting across from him.

"I'm here with some friends," I said. "We all went to dental school together."

"It's not Ashton, is it?" he asked with an easy smile.

His hair was really short, almost shaved. I wondered if he had it cut that way for a movie. I liked it—thought it looked good on him. I caught myself wanting to reach out and feel it—just rub my hand over the top of it so I could feel it between my fingers. I had to clear my throat before I could answer his question.

"Um, no. I'm uh, here with Kate, and our friends Victor and Charles."

"Victor and Charles, huh?" he asked, lifting his eyebrow slightly.

I glanced at Kate only to find that she was just staring at us with a comically confused look on her face.

"Hello Kate," Logan said, reaching out for a handshake.

She cleared her throat twice before saying, "Hi, hello, how are you? I'm a big, a really big fan of yours. I love your movies, and I used to watch Taylor and Tig like every day of my life."

He smiled and shook her hand. "I'm glad to hear it, thank you." Logan only smiled at Kate for a few seconds before turning his attention back to me.

"Rachel graduated at the top of our class," Kate blurted as soon as Logan looked away.

This caused him to smile and teasingly raise his eyebrows at me. "Is that so?"

I shook my head and rolled my eyes in a way that said, *it's probably true, but she shouldn't have said that.*

"So it's Doctor Stephens now?" he asked, looking impressed.

I bowed slightly, indicating that he was correct. "Our sushi's probably ready," I said, motioning to the dining room. It was the worst thing I could have said, but I was unreasonably nervous, and it just came out of my mouth before I could stop it.

"Seriously?" he asked, staring straight at me.

I smiled. "What?"

"I find you after all this time, and you're gonna talk about getting back to your sushi?"

I giggled nervously, and glanced at Kate who was wearing a look of shock.

"Please tell me you're planning on calling," he said.

I let my eyes roam over his face. He was wearing a sincere half-smile that took my breath away.

I nodded. "I, I, was actually. In September."

"I knew you would. I hoped you would have already done it by now. I thought you would have broken down."

My heart wanted to soar at the thought of him waiting for my call—until I remembered the blonde.

"We should both be getting back to our dates," I said.

"I'm not here on a date." He pointed at me. "Are *you* here on a date?"

The lady came out of the restroom. She almost walked off, but changed her mind and came back, asking Logan if she could take a picture with him. He graciously agreed and smiled while she held out her phone and took a selfie with him. She thanked him profusely and said what a big fan she was before heading back to her seat.

"Are you here with someone?" he repeated.

"Are you?"

"With my sister," he said. "You have to come to our table. I want her to meet you."

Kate, who was normally a calm person, let out a squeal at his words. We both glanced at her, and she smiled apologetically.

"Victor and Charles went to dental school with us," I said. "We're all just friends."

Logan and I shared a long stare. One in which I could not tell whether we were communicating a ton of things or nothing at all. It was a crazy feeling standing in the hallway staring at him like that. It was as if we were each trying to sync with one another... like we were scanning a radio to find a station where we could both meet up.

"I knew I'd find you before September," he said. The corner of his wide mouth curved upward in a confident grin.

"That's Charlotte you're with?" I asked.

I felt a rush of excitement at the news that he wasn't on a date after all. Logan had told me all about his sister that day on the hillside, and I loved having a face to go with the stories.

"You have to come meet her," he said with a jerk of his head in that direction.

Kate and I followed him. She made hilarious faces behind his back the whole time we walked, and it took every ounce of my restraint not to laugh. I saw her make eye contact with Victor and Charlie and make a face at them while pointing at Logan.

"Charlotte, this is Rachel and her friend Kate."

Charlotte smiled and stretched toward us from her seat, extending a hand for us to shake. I glanced at their table after I greeted her, and I couldn't help but notice that they were done eating.

Charlotte already seemed like a sweetheart, and all I had to go on was a smile and a handshake. Just like with her brother, there was something genuine about her. Living in a sea of people who wore fake smiles made you appreciate the real ones, and theirs were most certainly real.

"This isn't *Rachel*, Rachel, is it?" she asked, looking at her brother with great interest.

He smiled and nodded, and she instantly turned to me. Her whole posture fell as if she kicked into some other gear—relax mode. Her smile took on a whole new look as she stared intently at me. She stood and reached out for me. "Oh, honey, come here," she said. She was young and stylish, and hearing her call me honey in a warm, familiar way was a contradiction I had to wrap my brain around.

She hugged me tightly.

"I don't know what you did to my brother," she whispered. "But thank you." She squeezed, and I squeezed back.

"Rachel just finished dental school with honors," Logan said as Charlotte let me go and sat back in her chair.

She beamed at me once she got settled. "Logan was telling me about you doing dental school. That's awesome. Congratulations!"

"Thank you," I said. I couldn't calm down enough to appreciate the fact that she just said Logan had talked about me. Not to mention, I was pretty sure she referred to me as '*Rachel*, Rachel'.

"Kate just graduated, too," I said with a tilt of my head in Kate's direction.

"Congratulations to you, too!" Charlotte said.

"We're celebrating tonight," Kate said. "It's our first time to get together since we finished." She glanced at Victor and Charles, which made all of us do the same.

Our sushi had just arrived, and they had their backs to us, staring at the plates.

"I guess we should get back to our food," I said.

It was a tiny dining room, and everyone was sort of trying not to stare at us.

"Any chance we can just call it September?" Logan asked, holding up his palms.

"Please just call it September," Charlotte said.

I glanced at her curiously, wondering what exactly she knew about September.

She smiled at my expression. "You need to call my brother," she said. "I think you should really call him."

"You still have my number?" Logan asked, pulling out his chair and sitting casually on the edge of it.

I gave him a quick nod, and he smiled.

"Good. Maybe you can use it."

I smiled and nodded again. "It was nice meeting you," I said to Charlotte.

"You too," she said. "Call my brother!" she added, still smiling brightly.

Kate and I walked back to our place at the bar and sat down. "What on earth was that?" Victor asked quietly as we took our seats. "Did you just walk right up to them, or what?"

"I don't even know where I'm at right now," Kate said dazedly. She stared straight ahead like she was in some sort of trance. "I seriously can't believe that just happened to me," she continued. "Did that really just happen?" None of us said anything, so she continued, "Logan Ritchie just said all kinds of crazy *boyfriend* stuff to Rachel, and then his sister *hugged* her and acted like she was her long lost *best friend*." Kate paused and looked over Victor at me with huge eyes. "You were acting like you barely met him once, and he basically French kissed you and begged you to call him."

"He didn't do either of those things," I assured Charlie and Victor, who were listening intently to every word she said.

"He definitely begged you to call him," she said. "Even his sister was begging her. What in the world is going on here, Rachel? Am I dreaming?"

"Okay, is that really Logan Ritchie?" Victor asked.

None of us looked back, we just talked without really looking at each other in the process.

"In the flesh," I heard a deep voice say behind us. "You must be either Victor or Charles."

We all turned to find Logan and Charlotte standing right there behind us. Logan looked past us and smiled with a little two-fingered wave to the chef. "Thanks Tak," he said. He patted his stomach. "It was great." I turned and glanced over my shoulder to see the chef smile and bow at him.

"We're leaving," Logan said, making me once again turn to face him.

"We're just getting started," I said nudging my head toward the plate of sushi sitting behind me.

He nodded. "I just wanted to say goodbye."

"I'm glad you did," I said.

Before I could stop myself, I reached out and hugged him. The barstool made me almost as tall as he was, and I pulled him in before I could think better of it. He took me firmly in his arms before letting out a relieved sigh. He held me there for a few seconds sliding his hand onto the back of my head to press me close. The sensation of being held by him made my blood turn warm.

"I guess we can go ahead and call it September," he whispered close to my ear.

I pulled back far enough to look at him. "You think so?" I asked, smiling at him as we let go and I straightened on my stool.

"Yep," he said with that easy smile.

"It was so nice meeting you," Charlotte interjected, stepping forward to reach out for another hug.

"You too," I said.

Chapter 9

The four of us waved at Logan and Charlotte as they walked out of the restaurant. We had turned and were staring at our uneaten sushi when Kate said, "Did everyone just see what I saw, or am I trippin' right now?"

"I believe we did," Victor said.

She leaned forward and blinked at me as if she didn't know me at all—like I might be some strange person who swooped in and switched places with her friend.

I was laughing as I took a bite of salmon nigiri. I wasn't even hungry; I was just going through the motions of eating in an attempt to look like I wasn't freaking out on the inside.

"It seemed like you two were *really familiar*," Charles said. He and I were on opposite ends, so he leaned way over Kate to say it. His expression was totally serious, verging on grave, which made me giggle again.

"How do you know Logan Ritchie?" Victor asked.

"I got to go on a movie set one time."

"Why didn't you tell us about that?" Kate asked. "When was it?"

"It was last September, and I didn't tell you because it was no big deal. I didn't think it would amount to anything."

"He said he gave you his number," she said.

The boys were eating at this point, but Kate hadn't taken a bite, she was just looking past Victor at me.

"He did give me his number," I said, trying to act casual. I glanced at her to find that she was staring at me with an utterly dumbfounded expression.

"And you didn't *use* it?" she asked.

I let out another nervous laugh. "I told him I'd call him in a year," I said.

"A *year*? What in the world kind of crazy thing is that to say?"

I shrugged and shook my head in a self-deprecating way. "It was just a silly conversation we had," I said. "I thought he'd forget all about it."

"He did not forget!" she said with the widest of eyes. "He kept saying *'it's September'*, and I didn't know what he was talking about, but now that you say that, it all makes sense. He wanted you to call him." She paused. "Logan Ritchie wanted you to call him," she said wistfully.

Kate finally started eating, and the four of us sat there for the next thirty minutes while we finished up. The sushi lived up to the hype. It was a one of a kind experience to have a chef prepare what he wanted for me, and I enjoyed every bite of it. The taste of the food was probably enhanced by the fact that I was walking on air after seeing Logan.

Kate and the boys asked me lots more questions about him, but we eventually changed the subject to other things. It wasn't until the end of the meal that his name came up again, and that was on account of him buying our sushi. Our server enjoyed telling us that Logan had taken care of our check as an impromptu graduation gift, and we loved getting the news. My friends were all freaking out that Logan Ritchie had bought our dinner. We were so excited that everyone forgot I was supposed to buy ice cream. Charles and Victor had already taken off, and Kate and I were about to do the same.

"I hope you're gonna call him," Kate said, looking at me in the parking lot with an impassive stare. "Especially after he bought our dinner."

"I'll probably text him," I said, smiling.

She smiled and shook her head at me. "Smiling and acting all casual like it's no big deal..." she said, teasingly.

My smile broadened. "It's not a big deal," I said. "He's just a regular guy."

She tilted her head to the side and made a *who do you think you're kidding* face at me.

I laughed. "He is a normal guy," I said. "He puts his pants on one leg at a time like the rest of us."

I cringed inwardly at the phrase as it came out of my mouth, knowing I sounded just like my mom.

"I'm gonna kill you if you don't call him when you get home," she said. "And then call me to tell me what he said."

I smiled and shook my head at her. "I might."

"What? Call him or me?"

"Both. Either."

"You better at least call him. Promise you'll call him. He really wanted you to. It was so sweet."

"I probably will," I said, sitting in my car.

"You better!" she called as she sat in hers.

We smiled and waved at each other through the windows before starting our cars and pulling away.

***

I sat on my couch an hour later, staring at Logan's name in my contacts. He had simply put the name 'Logan' when he typed it in all those months ago. It wasn't my first time to stare at it, but this time I thought I might actually follow up by pushing some buttons. *Weren't there some set of rules I needed to follow with this? Should I wait two hours instead of just one? Should I wait a day or two—or maybe till September like I originally said? Would calling before September void my deal with God, or was it God who put him in my path tonight?*

I flopped my head onto the back of the couch, staring at the ceiling with a sigh. Then, all of a sudden, a peaceful feeling fell over me. Suddenly, I didn't care about the deal or September anymore. Suddenly, I was just a girl, and he was just a guy, and it was okay for me to talk to him. I unexplainably felt in my heart that I had no other option than to do so, and the sooner the better.

I started composing a text.

Me: "I can't believe I saw you tonight. Thanks so much for buying our dinner!"

I let my finger hover over the *send* button, hesitating only for a second before pushing it.

I started pressing random buttons on my phone, just because my fingers felt fidgety. I opened a couple of game apps and closed them again before setting my phone on the coffee table in front of me.

Within a minute, a phone call came in. Not a text, mind you, but a call—meaning I was about to be speaking with a live person. I saw as I picked up the phone that the person was Logan.

"Hello?" I said, doing my best to steady my voice.

"I can't believe you finally called me," I heard him say. "I thought you'd break down months ago."

"I'm patient to a fault, I guess," I said, with a smile in my voice. "I can't believe you bought our dinner."

"Where are you?" he asked.

I looked around. "My apartment, why?"

"I don't know, I guess I just want to see you again."

I laughed—not because what he was saying was funny, but more because I was just that happy.

"Because I want to see you again," he repeated. "I've been waiting for you to call for months, and if I don't see you tonight, it's gonna be at least another week." He didn't even give me a second to speak before he said, "Wait. That's it."

"What's it?" I asked. "You can come with us. You'll love it, and you'll get to meet the rest of my family."

"I am totally lost right now," I said.

Logan sighed as if trying to decide how to start at the beginning. "I'm leaving tomorrow to go to Myrtle Beach with my family. It's something we do every June. I was going to try to see you tonight before I left on my trip, but then I thought, *why can't she just come with us?*"

Gosh, it seemed like every time I talked to this guy, my stomach felt like it was cramped up into a tiny little jittery ball. *Was he asking me to take a trip with him?* It felt surreal, like I was misunderstanding the whole thing.

"Are you there?" he asked.

"Uh-huh," I replied.

"Did you hear what I said?"

"I think so."

"What do you think?" he asked. "What do you have going on right now?"

I hesitated for a few seconds. "I, uh, I'm, uh, just sort of taking a few weeks off before I head to Kenya and then start work."

"That's perfect! So, you're off right now?" he asked.

"Uh-huh," I said.

"Come with me," he said.

"To Carolina?"

"Yes. I think you're sort of supposed to since you happened to run into me on the perfect day for me to ask you. It's meant to be or whatever."

"Oh, is that what you think?" I asked. "What about September?"

"Screw September," he said with a smile in his tone. "I'm sorry, I shouldn't have said that, but seriously, September means nothing. I'd wait seven Septembers like he had to do for the Rachel in the Bible. I'd wait forever if I had to."

"Are you trying to woo me by comparing us to Bible characters?" I asked.

He chuckled. "I'm trying to woo you any way I can."

I laughed.

"So, you comin'?" he asked.

"I don't have a plane ticket or anything," I said. "I think it's kind of spur of the moment."

"So?" he asked.

"So I hadn't planned on picking up and flying across the country tomorrow."

"You said yourself you didn't have anything else going on."

"Yeaaah, I did."

"Great," he said as if it was all decided.

"Logan, I can't just go on vacation with you."

"Sure you can," he said.

I couldn't stop a huge smile from spreading across my face at how matter of fact he was being.

"Seriously?" I asked.

"Yes. Just pack. I'll take care of everything else. I'll call you back in a little while with details, but it'll be early tomorrow. We lose four hours going over there."

"Do I meet you at the airport or what?"

"I'll tell you all that when I call you back," he said. "I'll probably send a driver. Text me your address when we hang up."

"Okay," I said, feeling like everything was in slow motion.

"Okay, so I'll see you in the morning, Peaches."

"Peach cobbler?" I asked, remembering our conversation on the bench.

"The peachiest," he said, smiling.

"See you then," I said.

I smiled as we hung up, but it fell into a look of fear even though no one else was in my apartment. *What in heaven's name had I gotten myself into?* Logan had told me a story about his family's beach house back East, so I sort of knew to expect a huge family gathering. That, however, was all I knew. All sorts of thoughts and doubts crossed my mind, including thoughts of London and the fact that she lived in Myrtle Beach.

The reality of the situation had not sunk in yet, and I couldn't stop doubting that it was even true. One minute, I was eating sushi with some friends, and the next, I was packing my bags.

I made a conscious decision not to worry. Logan asked me, and I agreed to go, and that was all there was to it. Once I pushed my doubts and fears aside, they were replaced with excitement. I put on some music and began taking clothes out of my drawers and putting them into my bag.

"You excited?" he asked when I picked up my phone an hour later.

"I am," I said.

"Good. Your house isn't on our way to the airport, so I'm gonna send a driver for you, and you'll meet us there."

"Will he have my ticket? Or is it just under my name?"

"You don't need a ticket," he said. "Your driver will drop you off on the tarmac. You'll see where to go."

"Am I getting on a private jet?" I asked.

"Is that okay?"

"I guess it'll do," I said, teasing him.

"You probably got to ride in private planes all the time growing up."

I laughed. "Yeah, but there were chickens running around in there with us. Does your plane have chickens?"

"Maybe for lunch," he said.

We paused.

"I'm excited," I said. "Thank you for having me along. It's perfect timing. I'm trying to keep my toes in the sand for a few weeks to decompress from the last eight years of school."

"Now your toes and my toes can be in the same sand," he said. "Right next to each other."

I giggled. "My toes are wiggling around just thinking about it."

"My toes are wondering what took your toes so long to call," he said, smiling.

I let out another little laugh. "My toes thought your toes would forgot all about me by now," I said.

"I didn't," he said, with no mention of his toes. "Did you forget about me?"

"No."

"Did you wait for me?" he asked.

"What's that mean?"

"Have you been with anybody since we met?"

"Of course not," I said. "I told you where I stand on that."

"I don't mean sex. I'm talking about dating. Have you been seeing anyone?"

"No," I said, feeling nervous and jittery all over again. "Have you?"

"No." He answered quickly, which made me smile. "I've been busy with work. Plus, I promised you I'd wait."

"And you meant it?" I asked, although I phrased it like more of a statement.

"I meant it," he said. "Rachel?"

"Yeah?"

"Would you have called in September? You know, if I hadn't run into you tonight?"

"Yes," I answered. "Logan?"

"Yeah?"

"Would you have waited till September?"

"I told you that already. I would have waited as long as it took." He paused. "Actually, I would have given you till September, and then I would have gotten impatient and looked you up."

"Why didn't you already look me up?"

"Because you're the one who needed the whole September thing, not me. I was trying to respect that."

"Thanks," I said.

"You can thank me in person in the morning."

I smiled even though he couldn't see me.

"Your driver will be there at seven-thirty."

Chapter 10

A sleek black car was parked in front of my apartment when I went out at 7:23 the next morning. The driver got out as soon as I headed toward him.

"I'm sorry," I said. "I didn't know you were waiting."

"I just got here," he said. "I was about to call you." He was a lofty, middle-aged man wearing a suit. I wondered if he was part of some kind of service or if he specifically worked for Logan. "I'll take your bag, ma'am," he said.

His smile was so warm that I figured I'd ask him what was on my mind. "Do you work for Logan?"

"Today I do," he said with a smile. "It's my car. I work for other people, too, but Mr. Ritchie uses me quite a bit."

He opened the back door for me.

"Do you mind if I sit in the front with you?" I asked. I tried to glance into the passenger's side but couldn't see through the tinted windows.

"It's nicer back here," he said.

"Is it better for you?" I asked. "Is it part of your rules or something?"

He let out a hardy laugh. "No ma'am there's no rule on where you ride. I guess I'd like the company in the front, if it's all the same to you."

I smiled and nodded at him, and he reached out to open the front door instead. "Thank you... what's your name?"

"I'm Mike."

"Thank you Mike."

He smiled. "You're very welcome, Ms. Stephens."

Mike and I had a grand old time during the forty-minute commute to the airport. We talked about basketball, and Mexican food, and tons of other random things. He asked me how I knew Logan, and I told him a little about how we'd met. Mike had a lot of nice things to say about Logan, which made me feel proud.

We had to stop so he could talk to two different guards, but we were finally allowed to go onto the tarmac. I was already nervous, but my heart really started racing once I saw the plane he was headed toward. It was a small jet with a set of stairs pulled down and resting on the ground. There were two men standing near the stairs, but neither of them were Logan.

"That's the one?" I asked.

"Yes ma'am," he said as he pulled to a stop. "Stay put and I'll open the door for you."

"Logan was just going to call and see where you were," I heard one of the men say as Mike opened my door.

Mike smiled at him. "We left early and made good time," he defended.

I looked at the other man, who shrugged and smiled. "You know he gets in a hurry."

Mike went around to the trunk to get my luggage, and I followed him. "You must be Rachel," the same man called.

I gave him a little smile and wave but stayed back with Mike. "Yes sir," I said.

"And she's a little sweetheart, too, I'll tell you that right now," Mike said.

"You better keep your dirty, old paws off my lady," Logan said.

My heart stopped as I surveyed the scene, trying to find him. He was standing at the top of the stairs in the doorway of the plane, casually leaning on the handrails with a huge smile.

"You better mind your manners with this one," Mike warned, still teasing Logan.

Logan wore a huge, dazzling white smile as he put his hands up in surrender. "She won't tolerate anything *but* manners," he said.

I glanced at Mike, who winked at me and said, "Atta girl."

I smiled and popped up to kiss his cheek. "Thank you," I said. "I had fun." I handed him the twenty-dollar bill I had set aside for a tip, but he pushed it away without even looking to see what it was.

"Mr. Ritchie takes real good care of me," he said. "I appreciate it, though." He winked at me again and I tucked the bill into the back pocket of my jeans.

Logan had descended the stairs and was standing close to us by the time Mike and I had finished that exchange. "Why didn't you tell me you had me pickin' up a little doll this morning?" Mike asked Logan.

I blushed at the compliment, and Logan put his arm protectively around my shoulders. He squeezed me from the side, and reached over to place a kiss on my head. Mike began rolling my bag toward the two men who were talking, and Logan pulled me in that same direction.

"This is the pilot, Neil, and my dad, Robert," Logan said.

They both waved at me. Mike handed my bag off to Neil while Logan's dad crossed over to us. "This is Rachel," Logan said.

I stuck out my hand for Robert, but he went for the hug instead. "I pictured you blonde this whole time," he said, hugging me.

"Why'd you picture her blonde?" Logan asked.

His dad shrugged as he pulled back to stare at me. "I don't know, I guess because I have a blonde daughter, and you never said what color hair she has."

"He said she had dark hair," a woman called from the doorway of the plane where Logan had been standing. We all looked up at her, and she smiled and waved. She had brown, shoulder length hair, nice but casual clothes, and a warm smile. I could see a lot of Logan in her face, and I knew without a doubt that she was his mother.

"I'm Denise," she said, waving.

"Hey Rachel!" Charlotte yelled, peeking her head out of the plane behind her mom's shoulder. I smiled and waved at them both before glancing at Logan.

"What am I doing?" I whispered with a fearful smile.

"You're coming with me," he said.

"I guess I am," I said, sighing nervously.

"They're just big goobers like me," he said.

"How about everyone else?" I asked.

"Who?"

"You know, all your aunts and cousins and everyone."

"All goobers," he said with a smile. "Every last one of us. Even my grandma."

"Nothing to be afraid of, right?" I asked, psyching myself up.

"Nothing at all. You'll see."

***

There were only five passengers on the plane—Logan and I, along with his parents and sister. There was talk about his friend, Nico, coming along, but apparently, he wasn't able to at the last minute. It was a non-stop flight from L.A. to Myrtle Beach. We were in the air for about five hours. But we also lost four, so it was late in the afternoon by the time we arrived.

Logan had rented a massive SUV that was waiting for us when we arrived. Someone must've moved our luggage for us, because all we did was get off the plane and into the car without worrying about transferring anything.

"My oldest brother, David, and his family won't be there," Denise said as we drove to the house. "Their son and his wife just had their second baby a few days ago, so they're staying home this year."

"Logan said his grandma doesn't like it when you miss a year," I said.

Denise laughed at that. Robert was driving, and she smiled knowingly at him before turning to face those of us in the backseat. I was sitting in the middle between Logan and Charlotte, so she instinctually made eye contact with me.

"Mom's funny; you'll love her," she said. "She hates it when we have to miss, but she let Dave slide this year because of the baby."

"Is Evan gonna be there?" Logan asked.

"As far as I know," Denise said. She glanced at me. "Evan belongs to my brother, Dan," she explained. "He has three kids."

"Cody, Evan, and Mia," I said.

"You're good!" Denise said.

"I taught her on the plane while you were taking a nap," Charlotte said.

"And Logan had already told me a little about them when we first met," I added. "Hopefully, I can keep everyone halfway straight."

"Don't worry if you don't," Robert interjected from the front seat. "Denise and I were dating for two years before I got everyone's names right."

"It's not that hard," Denise assured me. "It'll be easy once you get there and meet everybody. Speaking of..." Denise said, trailing off as she looked at the side of Robert's face as he drove. "I haven't even thought about sleeping arrangements." She looked at me. "You might be on a couch," she said, reluctantly.

I shrugged. "I'm fine with that."

"She grew up in Kenya on a dirt floor," Logan said. I looked at him, and we shared a smile, both of us knowing good and well that I never slept on dirt floors.

"There might be enough bedrooms with Dave and Andy not being there," Robert said.

"Oh that's right," she said. "I'm sure there will be."

"I'm really not worried about it," I said. "A couch is fine with me."

"Yeah, I think she'd be fine upstairs on one of the couches," Logan said, with a sly smile that I knew meant he was trying to get me in his vicinity.

I squinted at him, and his smile broadened. He reached out and put his hand on my leg right above my knee. He gave me a little squeeze, letting his hand linger for a few long seconds. Even through the fabric of my jeans, I could feel the warmth.

"She can stay with Mia and I on the second floor," Charlotte said. "That's where all the cool kids stay."

"You should just mind your own business," Logan said, leaning forward.

Charlotte giggled. "Actually, the cool kids are upstairs," she said. "Maybe Mia and I will go up there and kick the boys downstairs."

"Maybe we'll just keep it like it is," Logan said.

We had several more minutes of this friendly banter before arriving at the house. I knew Logan had tons of money, so it shouldn't have surprised me, but the house was even better than I expected. It was a picturesque three-story place that was set up on piers. It was light green with white shutters and doors and was situated directly on the beach. I couldn't see the shore from the front of the house where we parked, but I could both hear and smell it, so I knew we were close.

"Logannnn! Charrrlotte!" a little girl yelled from the front porch as we got out. She was at the top of the stairs with the person I assumed was her mom.

"That's Cody's little girl, Ryan," Robert said, pulling our suitcases out of the back of the SUV one by one. "Paige is the girl standing up there with her. She's Cody's new wife."

"She's not the little girl's mom?" I asked, trying to get things straight.

"No." Robert smiled and winked at me, "but don't tell her that."

118

I smiled before glancing at the huge staircase that led to the front door. Logan was scaling the stairs in dramatic fashion, looking a bit slanky and janky like a long-armed ape.

Ryan stomped her feet and squealed with delight as she watched him coming to get her. She continued squealing as he made it to the top and took her into his arms, burying his face into her neck and cracking her up. After he had sufficiently tickled her, he positioned her on his hip as he came down the stairs.

Charlotte passed them on her way up, giving Ryan kisses on the cheek and making her crack up again. I watched them interact as I rolled my suitcase that way.

"I want you to meet my friend Rachel," Logan said, once he made it to the bottom of the stairs. I held out a hand to greet the little girl, but she lunged toward me with both arms extended as if wanting me to catch her. I dropped the handle of my luggage and set my purse next to my feet before reaching out to take her.

I let out a groan as I put her on my hip. "You got bigger since the last time I saw you!" I said.

She furrowed her eyebrows at me and scrunched up her nose.

My face broke into a grin as I tickled under her arm. "I'm just kidding; I never saw you before," I said.

"I knew I never did," she said, wagging her finger at me as if to say she was too smart for me to slip something past her.

"Hey punkin," Robert said, pinching at Ryan's leg as he passed with their luggage.

"Hi Uncle Rob," she said. "Did you meet Rachel before?"

"I sure did," he said.

"Did you bring her here?"

"Yep, she rode with us, but I think Logan brought her mostly."

Ryan stared at Logan, wondering if this was an accurate description of what happened.

He laughed. "She came with me," he said.

"Like your other friend?" she asked.

He shot her a curious expression, but then smiled as if he thought she was just confused. "Yep," he answered rather than explaining he had no idea what she was talking about.

She looked at me. "Did you meet my mom and dad?" she asked.

"Not yet."

"Did you meet my Memaw and Dee-dee?"

"I don't think so," I said. "I just met everyone who was in the truck with me."

"Did you get a haircut?" She asked Logan.

"I did," he said. He reached up and ran his hand through his freshly cropped hair. He could wear any hairstyle, but the super-short cut made him look tough and somehow mysterious. "I had to wear a wig for this job I just finished," he said. "And it's more comfortable like this."

"A wiiig?" she asked, laughing like it was a hilarious idea.

"Yep. A long wig like Uncle Evan's hair."

"Why didn't you let your real hair grow?"

"Because I didn't have time. It takes a long time to let your hair grow, and I couldn't do it before this job started."

"Granddad said uncle Evan needs to go buy a razor."

Logan laughed. "I'll bet he did."

She reached up, wanting to touch Logan's head, and he leaned over and let her do it. "Do you like it?"

"Uh-huh," she said, smiling with a big nod. She pulled back and glanced up at me. "Do you like to make sandcastles?" she asked.

"I love to make sandcastles," I said. "It's one of my most favorite things to do in the whole wide world!"

She wiggled around in my arms. "My daddy makes the best sandcastles ever, and you can help!"

Logan went to the back of the truck to get his bag, which was an oversized duffel. He came back with it hanging over his shoulder. "I'll get this," he said reaching out for my bag. He looked at Ryan. "Why don't you hold Rachel's hand up the stairs? And you can introduce her to everyone when we get in the house."

Chapter 11

"My uncle Evan smells like a goat," was the first thing Ryan said when we made it up the stairs to the front porch.

"I do not, you little booger!" a guy who I assumed was Evan said, scooping Ryan up and running into the house with her cracking up in his arms. Ryan's mom had been standing there watching the whole scene, and she was laughing as she watched Evan retreat into the house with her giggling daughter.

"I'm Paige," she said, extending her hand for me to shake.

I smiled and shook it. "Rachel," I said.

"Cody's my husband," she said. "He's Logan's cousin and Evan's older brother."

"And Evan's the goat that just stole your daughter?" I asked.

She laughed. "He's the free spirit of the family," she said. "Usually, when we first see him, he's fresh off of some environmental work, and hasn't bathed in days. This time, he had some dreadlocks I had to help him comb out. Don't worry, though. He's already had a shower."

The three of us were crossing the porch headed toward the door, and Logan turned to her. "Are we the last ones here?" he asked.

She nodded. "But Dave and Kathy aren't coming."

"Mom told us," Logan said. "She said Willow had her baby."

Logan reached out for the front door, but Paige stopped him by putting a hand on his forearm. "Somebody came by to see you," she said, in a quiet, concerned tone.

He cocked his head at her curiously, and she glanced at me regretfully. "We all remembered her from last year, and Cody and I saw her in California, so we just assumed you'd be okay with..." she trailed off before glancing at me again. "We didn't know you were bringing someone with you."

"What are you saying?" Logan asked, still seeming confused.

"That girl's here," Paige whispered, obviously feeling very awkward to say it in front of me.

"What girl?"

"London," I said, once I put all the pieces together.

"London's here?" he asked.

Paige nodded regretfully.

"Right now?"

She nodded again.

"Where is she?"

"I think she's on the deck with everybody. She acted like you were expecting her, so we let her in. I'm sorry."

Logan shook his head as we crossed the threshold into the house. We walked into a huge, open room that was a combination family room and kitchen. Denise and Robert were in there, along with a few others I didn't recognize.

"Who do we have here?" an older lady said from the kitchen as soon as she saw me come in. "Dee-dee, this is my friend Rachel," Logan said. He was smiling, but I could tell he was slightly on edge about the news of London's presence.

Paige left us alone and headed for the back door as the lady crossed to us with open arms. She hugged Logan first and then me. "It's so nice to meet you, Rachel! Any friend of Logan's is a friend of mine. My name's Diane, but they call me Dee-dee."

"You must be one of his aunts," I said.

"Oh my goodness," she said, taking me into her arms. "I love this girl already." She smiled at me. "I'm Logan's grandma, you precious little angel from heaven."

"She's the matriarch of this bunch," Logan said.

"Is this your house?" I asked.

"It's all of ours, but my name's on the title."

"It's gorgeous," I said.

"Thank you. We're glad to have you here. Make yourself at home."

"We're going to go get settled on the third floor," Logan said, taking a step toward the stairs.

"I think there's a bedroom open for one of you on the second floor if you want to look," Dee-dee said.

I really didn't care where I slept. I could concentrate on nothing but the fact that London was outside waiting for him. I felt nauseated. I followed Logan up the stairs, just doing my best to put one foot in front of the other. He had his duffel bag in one hand and my suitcase in the other. I didn't even think about asking him if I could help.

"You can hang out upstairs if you don't want to see her," he whispered as we walked. "I'll go down and tell her to leave and come get you when she's gone, if you want."

"You want me to?" I asked. "Do you think that would be best?"

"It's up to you," he said. "I just thought you could avoid her if you wanted to."

We came to the second floor and he stopped. "You can have the bedroom Dee-dee was referring to, or you can take one of the couches upstairs like we talked about."

"I'm good on a couch," I said. He smiled and continued walking to the third floor like that was what he wanted me to say.

The third floor boasted a big family room, similar to the one on the main level minus the kitchen. There were at least four couches and a few chairs spread over the room. Some of the seats were facing a TV, and others were facing the floor-to-ceiling windows on the back wall. You could clearly see the ocean from up there, and I gravitated toward the back wall to get a better look at it.

"Oh my gosh, this is so beautiful," I said walking slowly as I stared out the windows.

Logan set my bag next to one of the couches and his bag next to another. "Sometimes I sleep in a hammock with my cousins," he said.

"That's fine," I said. "I'm good right here as long as I'm not in anyone's way."

I moved to stand in front of my designated couch, and he came right next to me. He was several inches taller than me, and I stared up at him, feeling breathless. He had on khaki shorts and a fitted T-shirt that hugged every curve of his chest. Masculinity oozed out of him.

"Whatcha think?" he said.

"About what?"

"You wanna stay up here, or come with me?"

"What do you think I should do?" I asked.

He shrugged. "I want you to come with me," he said. "But I understand if you want to avoid her. I'm sorry this happened. I honestly thought I'd never see her again."

I wanted to ask if he'd been talking to her, but I didn't. He told me he hadn't talked to anyone, and I had to trust that.

"I guess I'll go down with you," I said.

"Really?" he asked, smiling.

"I guess."

"Good," he said. He grabbed my hand. "Let's go."

He held onto my hand for one flight of stairs, but let go before we made it all the way down. Even after he let go if it, I could feel where it had been, like it had left an impression on my skin. I was preoccupied by the feeling as I followed him across the first floor. It was a beautiful afternoon, and there wasn't a single soul in the house. We walked through the living room and kitchen, before opening the sliding glass doors to head to the sprawling deck.

It seemed as if the whole family was out there. Some were sitting in chairs, some were standing around a bar-b-que pit, and others were playing some tossing game. I had grown up around tons of people, but these were Logan's people, and I couldn't help but feel out of place—especially with London there.

"This is Logan's friend, Rachel," Ryan announced, pointing at us the second she noticed our arrival. "And I told you Logan had a haircut, see?"

Normally, I would have loved the sweet introduction, but I was trying not to make waves since I didn't know how London would react. I smiled and gave a little wave and curtsey to Ryan. I looked around, but didn't see London.

"We met Rachel already," Dee-dee told her great-granddaughter.

"I didn't," a guy said. He waved from the other side of the deck. "Cody," he added.

I figured as much since he was standing right next to Paige.

"I'm Logan's Aunt Christy, and this is his Uncle Dan," a lady said from her chair.

I smiled and waved at her. "It's nice to meet you," I said.

"*Rachel?* Rachel Stephens? Is that you?" London's voice came from the right hand side of the deck. She was totally shocked, I knew that before I even looked at her and saw that her jaw was hanging open.

The deck was up on piers just like the rest of the first story, and London was standing at the top of the stairway that led to the ground as if she had just walked up. Obviously, she missed our initial appearance because she came to stand in front of us with a comically confused look on her face.

"What are you doing here?" she asked. "Did you come here to see me?"

I couldn't stop a little laugh from leaving my lips. *Did she just ask if I came to see her?*

"She's here with me," Logan said.

London looked back and forth between us for several painfully long seconds. "She's here with *you?*" she asked with a revolted look on her face.

"Yes," he said.

"She, Rachel Stephens, came here with you, Logan Ritchie?" she asked.

"Yes, London, she's here with me."

128

She coughed out a laugh. "Are you kidding me right now?" she asked.

"Did she ride on a *plane* with you?" Her tone was increasingly agitated.

"How else would she get here?" he asked.

Her eyes were like daggers when she turned to face me again. "Did this happen last year?" she asked, referring to her trip.

I said, "No."

But at the exact same time, Logan said, "Yes."

"Which is it?" she asked, angrily. "Did it or didn't it?"

Out of the corner of my eye, I saw Paige heading down toward the stairs with Ryan on her hip. I felt bad for making a scene even though I wasn't the one getting upset.

"We haven't seen each other since the last time I saw you," Logan said, honestly. "I ran into her at a sushi bar yesterday and invited her to come with us."

"Then why'd you just tell me you hooked up with her last year?" she asked.

"Because I wish we would have," Logan said. "She was too nice to let anything happen. She was worried about you."

She just stood there and stared at us with an annoyed look on her face. "Some kind of friend you are," she said, glaring at me as if she hadn't just heard what Logan said in my defense.

My instinct was to apologize, but I couldn't make myself do it. I wasn't sorry. I just gave her a regretful smile and watched as she pushed past me and into the house. We all assumed she was leaving even though she didn't say as much.

"He always did have a flair for drama," Christy said, making everyone crack up once London was inside with the door closed behind her.

"I'm sorry about that," Cody said. "That was my fault. I'm the one who let her in."

"You didn't know," Logan said.

"We should have known she wasn't your girlfriend," a girl said from her chair. "She's not your type at all."

"What do you know about my type, Mia?" Logan asked.

The two of them smiled as they met in the middle of the deck and embraced. She squeezed him tightly, groaning with the effort. He gave her a nuggie on the head, and she pushed at him with a huge grin.

"I knew she wasn't," Mia said, referring to the question about his type. "This is more like it," Mia said with a smile and a hand extended in my direction.

"This is Rachel," Logan said.

I shook her hand. "Nice to meet you, Mia."

"We're having a girl's day tomorrow if you wanna come," Mia said.

"I forgot about that, or I would have already told her," Charlotte chimed in. She was playing a game with Evan on the far side of the deck. There was a metal ring hanging from a string attached to the trellis, and it looked as though they were trying to rope it onto a hook that was affixed to the house.

"You forget because you don't *need* a spa day," Evan said, teasing Charlotte. "Every day of your life's a spa day in Cali."

She pushed at him playfully, and he tickled her like she was a little kid. They were so cute; it made me wish I had been closer to my cousins growing up.

"Wanna go down to the beach?" Logan asked, looking at me.

"Plan on coming with us tomorrow," Mia said, sitting in one of the chairs.

I smiled and nodded at her before regarding Logan. "A sandcastle?" I asked.

"An epic one," he promised.

He glanced at his cousin. "Cody we might need your help," he said.

Cody smiled and nodded, obviously overhearing us. "Paige probably has Ryan down there already. I'll be down in a minute."

Logan grabbed my hand, leading me down the stairs to the sand below. "Hang on," I said when we got to the bottom. I put my hand on his shoulder, using him for balance as I reached down to pull off my sneakers and socks.

"Me too," he said. He waited for me to finish before kicking off his sandals. "You can just leave them here," he said, seeing that I was planning on carrying mine with me.

I dropped them next to his sandals.

"You look good at the beach," he said, letting his eyes roam over me.

I smiled shyly. "You're not so bad yourself."

"I can't believe you're standing right in front of me," he said. "I've been talking myself out of believing you were real."

"Why would you go and do something like that?" I asked.

"I hope I'm not interrupting," Cody said, coming down the stairs.

"Heyyy," we heard from the direction of the beach. "We were just coming to get you guys."

I looked that way to find Paige and Ryan.

"You guys have the shovels and pails?" Logan asked seeing that everyone was empty handed.

"It's all down there," Cody said, motioning to the beach.

Chapter 12

We walked as a group toward the sound of crashing waves. There was a stretch of deep, soft sand with a path through some shrubs and bushes before we made it to the shore.

"This is our beach!" Ryan yelled, holding out her arms as if introducing me to the water.

"I love your beach," I yelled back, smiling at her.

"Did you ever see a beach before?"

I nodded. "I've seen lots of beaches."

"Did you see this one?"

I nodded, thinking back to the time when we visited Myrtle Beach to do some fundraising at the Ryder's church.

"What do you do," Paige asked, pulling me from my thoughts.

Logan and Cody were already pointing at the sand, marking off the area for our sandcastle, and I smiled absentmindedly at the sight of them getting so into it.

"I just graduated dental school," I said.

"With honors," Logan added.

"Wow!" Paige said, sweetly. "A dentist, huh? I don't think I know any dentists," she shrugged, "except for the one I go to."

"I go to the dentist," Ryan said, showing me her smile. "And I have a loose tooth!"

I gave her a big, excited smile. "You do? That's so exciting."

"Is it your first one?"

"Yeah."

"Yes ma'am," Cody corrected from a few feet away.

"Yes ma'am," Ryan said. She was actively shoveling sand into a pail as she spoke.

"I think those are very nice manners," I said, causing Ryan to glance at me and smile. "I'm gonna be a kids' dentist when I start work, and I hope all of my patients have nice manners like you."

"I can be your patient if you want me to."

"She works all the way out in California," Paige said, sitting next to Ryan to begin scooping. She looked at me. "I assume that's where you live," she amended.

I nodded as I grabbed a shovel and pail and followed their lead, not even caring that I still had jeans on. "Your mama's right, I work way out west next to a different beach."

"Or in Kenya," Logan said.

This caused Paige to give me a curious glance.

"My parents have a rescue center over there," I said. "I'll travel there and run clinics a couple times a year."

"What kind of rescue center?"

"It's for kids who have nowhere else to turn," I said. "Orphaned, neglected, abused, left behind... they all have a different story."

"What ages?"

"They come to us at all different ages—we've had some come as babies, but others show up on our doorstep in their teens. Most of them from really tragic situations."

"What's tragic?" Ryan asked.

"It means they had something hard or sad happen to them."

"But then they got happy again?" Ryan asked, peering up at me.

"Yep, they sure do get happy again," I said. "I got to grow up over there, so I saw kids go from sad to happy tons of times."

"That's so cool," Paige said, staring off as if trying to imagine what it must have been like. "Can we look it up online?" she asked.

"Oh, of course," I said. "My parents would love for you to take a look at it. They're always trying to get the word out. They've really expanded over the years. It's amazing to see what God's doing. My mom started out with three little girls in a tiny house, and it's grown to homes, and farms, and schools on three different locations."

"And we can see it and read about it online?"

"Oh yeah, they have a Facebook page and everything."

"That's so cool," Paige said. "I don't think I've ever known a dentist or a missionary, and now I meet a dentist missionary."

135

I laughed. "I probably only deserve the first title since I only plan to make trips over there. I'll be the regular dentist and let my parents do the hard stuff."

"Don't let her fool you," Logan said, as he and Cody began transporting sand to our castle site. "She's doing the hard stuff—just not always in Kenya."

"It's really not hard," I said.

"What?" Paige asked.

I shook my head and smiled like I was embarrassed he had mentioned it. "It's really not hard," I repeated. "He's just talking about a free clinic I'll be doing." I continued to scoop sand into my pail. "What about you?" I asked Paige. "What do you do?"

"I'm in beauty school right now," she said.

By instinct, used the back of my forearm to brush some hair off of my forehead. I smiled when I did it.

"What?" Paige said, noticing my amusement.

"I started adjusting my hair when I heard that's what you did, and it made me think about how people always check their teeth when I tell them what I do."

Paige laughed. "No doubt!" she said, "I'm sitting over here using my tongue to make sure I don't have anything stuck between my teeth as we're talking."

"Me too," Cody said, causing everyone else to laugh.

Cody was the official foreman of the sandcastle crew. He gave us instructions about what goes where before jumping in to help us. It was going to be four or five feet tall, which was by far the largest sand structure I'd ever been a part of building. I would have turned two or three buckets over and called it a day, but they were apparently professionals. Cody had a grown-up shovel out there along with a few other tools that I was relatively sure came from his real job as a stonemason.

Logan and Cody both had their shirts off the whole time. I had Googled Logan enough times to know what he looked like without a shirt, but being in close proximity to the actual muscles as they moved and flexed was totally different. I did my best not to look, and when I did, it wasn't for more than a few seconds at a time.

We worked on the castle for what must have been about an hour before Dee-dee came out to the beach with Mia and Charlotte. "Y'all are missing out," Mia yelled as they approached.

"Burgers and hotdogs are ready," Dee-dee clarified. "We already ate."

They came to stand near our castle and started taking it in. "I didn't know you were making one this magnificent," Dee-dee said.

"Why's it have a big tooth?" Mia asked, "Is that what that is?" She walked around, staring at it intently.

"Because it's the Tooth Fairy's castle!" Ryan announced, jumping and squealing in the process. "Ms. Rachel's gonna pull my tooth, and the Tooth Fairy's gonna come see me tonight!"

Diane stared at Ryan with wide-eyes. "Do you have a loose tooth?"

Ryan nodded and stretched up, opening her mouth in all sorts of funny ways to let her great grandmother get a look inside. "It's the bottom," she said. Her mouth was still open wide and contorted, so it sounded more like, "Iii uhh aah um."

"Ohhh!" Dee-dee said, seeming impressed even though she had no idea what Ryan was saying.

"It's the one on the bottom," Paige clarified.

"Ohhh!" Dee-dee said again, even more impressed this time. "That's amazing! The Tooth Fairy's gonna love her castle."

"Uh-huh," Ryan said.

Paige stood up and started dusting herself off. "We might need to put it on hold for a little while and get you some dinner."

Logan had gotten really sandy, so he stood as well and began rubbing his own legs, backside, and arms. I, on the other hand, still had on my jeans and blouse from the flight and had made a real effort not to get sandy. I had been standing and squatting the whole time, so my jeans were nearly sand-free. I pretended to be watching Cody smooth the castle walls, but out of the corner of my eye, I could see Logan brushing off the sand, and then bending down to grab his T-shirt. I snuck a for real glance at him when he lifted the shirt over his head and shrugged into it. He'd been hitting the gym; there was no doubt about it. I stood up straight and rolled my shoulders back instinctually.

"Whatever happened with you and that guy?" Logan asked, looking at Mia. She was standing next to Dee-dee staring at her phone, and she smiled at Logan. "We still talk a little bit," she said, stashing her phone in her pocket.

"Travis Guinn," Charlotte said in explanation to me. "He lives about half a mile that way." Charlotte pointed down the beach, and I craned my neck that way even though there was no way I could see what she was talking about.

"We met him when we were here last year," Mia explained. "I talked to him a little bit once I got back to Charlotte, but I was busy with school, and he's busy with work, so it just sort of fizzled out."

"Are you gonna try to see him while you're here?" I asked.

Everyone looked at Mia like they were curious about that as well.

"I might," she said, shrugging. "I'll probably text to let him know I'm in town at least. He might be having another party like last year."

"I don't know if I'd go," Charlotte said. "I ended up with the douchebag of the bunch that night." She sighed as she looked at me. I was the only one who didn't know what she was talking about, so she explained, "I wasted my whole night talking to an Australian guy, and at the end of it, he tells me he's got a girlfriend back home."

"Did he kiss you?" Cody asked.

"No," she said as if it was none of his business.

"Did he lead you on somehow?"

She hesitated. "Not really."

"Then why's he such a douchebag?"

"Because he was super hot and super sweet," she said, sticking out her bottom lip. "I loved his accent, and I wanted him to break up with his girlfriend for me."

Everyone laughed including Charlotte, who knew she was being ridiculous. We all stashed the tools in a big pile and began walking down the sandy path that led to the house.

"What if you get in touch with Travis and he said he's having another party?" Charlotte asked as we walked.

"Then I guess we'll go," Mia said. "If everybody wants to. What if Sam's there again? Will you go?"

"Probably not. It'd just be torture."

Logan was walking next to me. I didn't chime in at all. I knew from things I'd already heard that Logan met London at that party, and it gave me a queasy feeling just hearing them talking about it. Logan and I fell to the back of the pack as we walked toward the house.

"I can't believe I still have on my jeans," I said, dusting them off a little even though they were mostly clean.

"I kept thinking you were gonna go in and change," he said.

"I kept meaning to, but I didn't want to abandon my duty to the Tooth Fairy."

He glanced at me as we walked. "You and the Tooth Fairy must be pretty tight."

I nodded. "We have a working relationship. It wouldn't be right for me to cut out on the construction of her home just to go change out of my jeans."

"You did the right thing," Logan said in all seriousness. In that moment, I could see him as an actor, and appreciate how natural he was at it.

Paige, who was walking right in front of us, glanced back with a smile as if she enjoyed listening to our conversation. She and Cody were holding hands as they walked, and I caught myself looking at them. I knew it was good to be content, and I did the best I could, but I wanted what they had. I really did long to find my perfect partner. I hoped I hadn't messed this one up by not waiting till September.

Logan's uncle Dan had grilled the burgers. I didn't think I was hungry, but it was so delicious that I ate the whole thing, and it was huge. They had all sorts of toppings like mushrooms, avocado, sprouts, and about ten different types of cheeses and condiments to choose from.

Logan stayed at the house with me to change clothes after we finished eating. The others had gone back down to the beach to finish the sandcastle.

"How long have you known Logan?" Diane asked when he and I were crossing the deck to head downstairs.

We both stopped in our tracks to speak to her. I looked at him with a smile before answering. "We met last year, but we lost touch for a while."

"I wouldn't call it *losing touch*," he said with a teasing expression aimed at me.

I widened my eyes at him, and he laughed as he looked at his grandma, pinching me lightly with his knuckles in the process. "She's a good girl, Dee-dee, and she wasn't so sure about me at first."

I smiled, but widened my eyes playfully at him again like he was putting me on the spot.

His smile grew bigger. "I'm trying to convince her I'm a good catch, so everybody please do your best to talk me up when I'm not around."

Dee-dee along with the four or five other people who were out on the deck all laughed, and I giggled right along with them.

"Logan is an excellent catch," Dee-dee said.

"I don't doubt it," I said, still smiling even though I was nervous.

"You're supposed to wait till I'm not around, Dee-dee," Logan said, teasing his grandma.

She held her hands up in surrender. "I just call it like I see it," she said.

Chapter 13

Logan and I saw Paige and Ryan coming up the stairs when we got to the top of them to head down.

"Can you please pull my tooth so my mom can take a picture of me with it before it gets dark?" Ryan asked.

Paige smiled hopefully at me. "You don't have to."

I nodded and motioned to them to come up. I held my hands out when they reached the top, and Ryan threw herself willingly into them. I settled her on my hip, and she held on tightly with all of her limbs, squeezing me especially hard with her legs. I knew just by the way she held onto me that she was excited.

"You must be a monkey," I said.

She laughed. "I'm just nervous, and I clanched on."

It was weird hearing such a little girl admit to being nervous, but the part of that statement that stood out to me was the word *clanched*. I stood there and stared at her. "Did you just say 'clanched'?" I asked with a serious but entertained expression.

Ryan looked at me with those big brown eyes and nodded.

"Where'd you hear that word?" I asked.

She shrugged.

"She makes up words all the time," Paige said.

"Did you just make up 'clanched'?" I asked.

She smiled and nodded. "Because it feels like clanching when I squeeze you real tight like this." She squeezed her legs extra hard, and I faked in a silly way like I was in pain. Ryan cracked up, which made everyone else laugh, too. Clanching was exactly what I wanted to do with Logan. We had scarcely made any physical contact, and I felt like I needed a good clanch.

"Welcome to my office, ma'am," I said, setting her on the kitchen counter next to the sink. Her feet swung back and forth as they dangled. She took a deep, nervous breath as she smiled at me with her eyes wide open. I couldn't help but let out a laugh at the precious sight. "You are just about the cutest patient in the whole world," I said.

Paige and Logan were already standing there watching, but Dee-dee and Cody's mom, Christy, came in to catch the action as well.

"You mind if we watch?" Christy asked.

Ryan held her mouth and eyes wide open as she shook her head stiffly.

"You can relax for a second," I said, smiling as I patted her on the leg. "Can you sit up here all by yourself if I go get a few things?"

Ryan nodded.

Diane had already showed me where there was a box of latex gloves, so I washed my hands before pulling them out of the cabinet and filling a glass with water. I talked to Ryan the whole time I got prepared. I said things to build her trust and confidence and make her laugh. Finally, I came to stand in front of her and pulled on the gloves. "These are a little grippy," I said, rubbing my finger and thumb together to demonstrate. "Do you mind if I just wiggle your tooth a little bit?"

She shook her head, but I could tell she was nervous. She opened her mouth, and I gently touched her tooth. "I'm not going to try to get it just yet, but you should know that once I do, it's going to be really easy."

"It is?" she asked, looking a little less intimidated.

I smiled and nodded, looking straight at her. "It's really, super loose," I said. "You'll barely even notice when it comes out."

"Okay just do it, but what if it hurts?"

"I can just about promise it won't hurt," I said. "And the Tooth Fairy's really gonna like this one. It's nice and white."

She nodded.

"Can I wiggle it again, maybe just a little more this time?"

She nodded and pushed her precious little lip out to let me access the tooth.

"And if I happen to take it out, that'd be okay too, right?" As I was saying the words *that'd be okay too, right*, I pulled the tooth.

Ryan was nodding as an answer to my question when I held it up for her to inspect.

I smiled and handed her the glass of water. "It's a beauty!" I said.

"It is?" she asked, beaming at me.

I nodded. "Take a sip of this water. Swish it around, and spit right here in the sink if you want."

She did as I said, leaning over the sink to spit. "I swallowed some," she said.

"That's okay." I rolled up half a paper towel and handed it to her. Bite down on that for a few seconds."

"Is it bleeding," she asked in that muffled way people speak when they're biting down on something.

"Barely," I said. "It was ready to come out."

I handed the tooth to Paige.

"Daddy's gonna want to see this," she said, staring down at it as if it was a priceless artifact.

Ryan smiled past the paper towel, and kicked her feet excitedly.

"You were such a big girl," Logan said.

She made pretty eyes at him, which was a combination of different types of blinks. They passed the tooth around as I cleaned up my mess.

"Let me see," I said, coming to stand by her. She took out the makeshift gauze and let me inspect the hole where her tooth had been. "It'll probably feel funny for a little while, but that's part of the fun of losing a tooth. I think you're fine to stop using that." I pointed to the paper towel. "You can take a sip of water if you want."

"How about a popsicle?" Christy asked.

"A popsicle might taste good," I said.

I took the tooth from Paige with the intention of showing it to Ryan and telling her how nice it was. I spotted a notepad on a catchall section of the countertop. I knew no one would mind if I used it, so I went over and picked it up along with a pen that was sitting nearby.

"Nurse Dee-dee, can you hand me a Ziploc bag, please."

"Yes, ma'am I can," Dee-dee said, playing along.

"Doctor," she said, bowing slightly as I dropped the tooth into the bag she held open.

I bit the inside of my cheek to keep from laughing. I handed the baggie to Ryan with a similar bow to the one Dee-dee had just given me, and she went right to work staring at it. She was getting a good look at it when Christy handed her a popsicle.

I wrote the words "Patient" and "Tooth" on the paper, and added a line at the bottom as a place to sign my name. I turned where Ryan could see the paper from over my shoulder. "This is my official report," I said. "You get an A-plus for being a good patient, and an A-plus on your tooth." I wrote the grades with a flourish before scribbling my fancy signature on the line. I ripped off the paper and handed it Ryan. "Make sure the tooth fairy gets this," I said. I winked, and Ryan wiggled with excitement.

"I lost a tooth!" she yelled as Evan came through the back door.

"Get outta town!" Evan said. "Let me see."

She showed him her big smile, and he whistled.

"That looks beautiful!" he said.

"And I got two A-pluses!"

"A-pluses in what?" he asked.

"In patience and tooth," she said proudly, even though she didn't quite understand.

"That's amazing. Did your dad see?"

"We're going to show him right now," Paige said. She helped Ryan down from the counter and then dropped the paper with Ryan's grades into the Ziploc with the tooth. "We gotta get a picture of you next to that castle," she said. "Maybe Ms. Rachel will come take a picture with you."

I nodded.

"We'll be down there in a few," Logan said.

Most everyone followed them out—everyone except for Evan who announced he was hungry for something sweet and was digging in the fridge.

"Can you be my dentist?" Logan asked.

I stood right in front of him with a smile. "Sure," I said. "I'll be seeing some adults—I just *mostly* see children."

"Logan's a child," Evan said, without looking at us.

"Older than you, son," Logan said. It took him all of three seconds to grab a nearby dishcloth and take a shot at whipping Evan with it. It wasn't much of an effort because he knew it wouldn't reach.

"Aunt Denise said you save the world and whatnot," Evan said, leaning against the counter casually as he crossed his legs in front.

"I heard *you're* the one saving the world," I returned.

He shrugged confidently. "I do what I can," he said, obviously teasing. It was the same sarcastic sense of humor Logan had. It reminded me of my brother, which was why I clicked so well with them. "Logan plays some charity golf," Evan said, still ribbing his cousin.

"I don't have to explain my charity work to you," Logan said.

"What work?" Evan said.

"He thinks my job is easy," Logan said confidently. "I just let him believe it. It helps his confidence."

Evan laughed. "I'm just messing with you. Mom told me you gave like a million dollars to the EOC. Thank you for doing that." Evan wore a sincere smile, and Logan gave him a quick nod, which I took as a *you're welcome*.

"Plus, I'm going to Kenya in a few weeks," Logan added. My head whipped around to stare at him, and he smiled, looking my way.

"Are you talking about coming with me?" I asked.

He smirked and shrugged.

"Is it even a possibility?" I asked.

He shrugged again, this time with a nod. "I'm not working right now."

"I told you he doesn't work," Evan said, eating a spoonful of yogurt from its plastic container.

"Thank you from the peanut gallery," Logan said without glancing at Evan.

I laughed. I felt a whole host of emotions at the thought of Logan coming with me. I was leaning against the counter, and he stood close to me—our arms close enough to feel each other's body heat.

"Would you really think about doing something like that?" I asked.

"I'd love to do it," he said. "Are you inviting me?"

"Of course!" I said. "Of course you're invited." I paused. "I can't believe you'd *want* to do something like that."

"I can," Evan said sweetly. "I know what sort of stuff my cousin does when he thinks nobody's looking. I'm just messing around when I say otherwise."

"I didn't even pay him to say that," Logan said, with a jerk of the chin in Evan's direction.

"My mom would flip her lid if you came to the center," I said. "Her Facebook page would be blowing up left and right." I paused. "No pressure or anything, though."

"I'm the one who invited myself," he said.

"And you think you might be able to really come?"

He nodded.

"I'm excited," I said, smiling broadly at him.

"I am too," he said.

"Now y'all got me wantin' to go to Kenya!" Evan said.

"The more the merrier," I said. "My parents will put you to work in a heartbeat."

"Don't you have some whales to save?" Logan asked.

Evan pointed at me. "She said they needed help, dawg."

"Do they?" Logan asked.

I smiled at how sweet and sincere he was. "They can always use help," I said. "They'll have no problem putting you to work. It takes a lot to keep that place running."

Logan smiled at Evan. "You can come with us if you want," he said.

"You payin'?" Evan asked.

Logan nodded easily.

"I'm in," Evan said, clapping his hands together. "Let's do this."

"It'll be fun," Logan said.

"I'm stoked! When is it? Three weeks?"

I nodded.

"You sure you're all right with this?" Logan asked, looking at me.

"I'm thrilled," I said. "If you two really come with me, my mom's gonna love me forever."

"Why didn't you ask me sooner?" Logan asked, turning his whole body to face me.

"Because I never dreamed you'd really go."

"He'll go," Evan said, confidently. "He doesn't say he'll do something unless he's serious."

"I didn't pay him to say that either," Logan said.

"He's just trying to make up for how much he made me dislike you at first," I said, smiling.

Evan cracked up, and Logan popped him with the towel, this time not missing.

"Ouch!" Evan said.

"You sort of deserved it," I said, still smiling at Logan.

"Thank you!" Logan said.

"She's sweet on you, cuz," Evan said.

"No, she's just smart, and she can see who's being reasonable and who's not."

"I am sort of sweet," I said.

When I started speaking the phrase, I planned on saying "I am sort of sweet *on you*," but the words "on you," got stuck in my throat and wouldn't come out, so I just said, "I am sort of sweet."

Logan cocked his head at me slightly and gave me a teasing grin. "You're sweet? Or you're sweet *on me*?" he asked, calling me out.

I blushed. I could feel blood rise to my cheeks. I put my head in my hands and giggled. "Just plain sweet," I said, feeling mortified and wanting to get out of the pickle I was in. "I'm just plain old sweet."

"Oh, because for a second there I thought you were gonna say you were sweet *on me*."

"I thought she was, too," Evan agreed, wearing a look of mock confusion. They were both wearing deadpan expressions as they stared at me. *A family of clowns,* I thought.

"I wish that's what she was saying," Logan said, acting disappointed.

I leaned to the side to bop him with my hip. "I was maybe going to say that, but you two clowns had to get me all red-faced and embarrassed."

Logan put a hand on my shoulder and brought me in for a tiny hug. "I like you embarrassed," he said. "It's cute."

"It's not to me."

He poked at my ribs, and I pulled away from him. I narrowed my eyes and pointed a finger at him. "The only thing that could make matters worse is if you tickle me," I said, sincerely. "I whole-heartedly *hate* being tickled. I can't stand it. I seriously get mad when people try to tickle me."

I saw Logan make a jerking motion. He flexed his hand and then stared at it with a confused expression like he couldn't control what was happening to him. He flexed it again.

"Don't you even think about it," I warned as I took a step back.

He had that *I'm about to tickle you* look in his eyes. I had a brother. I knew all about that look.

"Seriously, I will get so mad at you," I said.

Just a tiny one," he said, reaching out toward my ribs.

"No!" I squealed, jumping back. "I hate it."

"You know when you say something like that, you make it impossible for him *not* to do it, right?" Evan asked.

I glanced at Logan with fear in my eyes, and he shrugged as if he wasn't responsible for his own behavior.

Chapter 14

Logan chased me into the living room. I circled around to the front of one of the sofas, and he stared at me from the other side of it with a wild-eyed expression.

"Don't," I said. I was pointing a finger at him, but I couldn't help but smile, which he took to mean I wasn't all that serious.

His eyes widened like something was coming over him and he had to tickle something before he exploded.

I squealed and backed up, but he was already going through the motions of advancing on me. Using a hand on the back of the couch for leverage, he jumped over the sofa, landing nimbly on the other side. I ran, but there was no getting away. He was athletic and fast, and he knew this living room like the back of his hand. He scooped me into his arms and swung me around, causing me to fall onto the sofa.

I giggled like a little girl, which turned to belly laughing as his fingers expertly tickled my ribs. I laughed hard every time I got tickled—the good kind of laugh where you barely even make a sound aside some wheezing. Logan had one knee on the couch as he hovered over me.

"Pleeease!" I managed to say, although it was nearly inaudible.

He stopped, and I was finally able to take a deep breath. I scooted up just a little with my arms tucked to my chest defensively. "You made me ugly laugh," I said, with a teasing grin.

"There was nothing ugly about that laugh," he said. He was still hovering over me and was almost whispering. Even if Evan was still sitting in the kitchen, it was likely that he couldn't hear us.

"I'm mad at you for that," I whispered.

Logan shot me a challenging smile. "You are?"

The answer was no.

I wasn't mad at all. Getting tickled was a small price to pay for ending up with him staring down at me like this. I wanted him to kiss me. I looked at his mouth. His gorgeous lips curved upward in a devastatingly handsome smile. I remembered what they felt like that day on the concrete bench, and I took an unsteady breath at the memory.

"Are you?" he asked, still waiting for me to say whether or not I was mad.

"I'm not *that* mad," I narrowed my eyes. "But that doesn't mean I want you to do it again."

We stared at each other for a few seconds. "I can't believe you pulled my little cousin's tooth," he said. "That was the most adorable thing I've ever seen."

"I know," I said. "She's the cutest little girl."

He smiled at me. "I wasn't talking about her."

I squirmed a little at the compliment. It made me nervous to see him staring down at me like that. I glanced at his neck, and chest and anything else besides his face—his mouth, the mouth I wanted so desperately to be on mine.

"Are y'all coming?" we heard a woman's voice say as the glass door slid open.

I couldn't see who it was from where I was laying, but Logan peeked over the back of the couch in that direction and smiled.

"We're coming," I heard Evan say.

I stared up at Logan, who nodded toward the person who was talking. "I think Ryan wants a picture with Rachel by the sandcastle," the lady said.

I scooted out from under Logan and sat up on the couch. "I'm on my way out there," I said. I glanced at Logan with a smile as if asking him to move so I could stand up.

He answered my unspoken question with a shake of his head.

"No?" I asked.

He shook his head again.

"Why not?"

He shrugged. "I just want a few more seconds."

"Of what?" I asked.

"You."

"You've got me all week," I said.

He smiled. "Not like this."

I couldn't believe I'd seen this guy in movies, and now he was staring at me like I was a leading lady. My heart was fluttering a million miles an hour. He stared at me for a few more seconds, and

157

just like that, he stood, extending a hand to help me get up as well. No kiss—not even a little peck on the cheek or anything.

"I'm not sorry for tickling you," he said, once I got to my feet. I glanced toward the kitchen to see that Evan had already gone outside. Logan and I were alone.

I had to clear my throat before I could speak. "You should be sorry," I said, squinting at him.

"But I'm not," he said. He pulled me into his arms and squeezed me tightly. His chest was broad and firm, just begging me to rest my face on it. I did so and hugged him back while I was at it.

"I'm trying to be really mad at you right now for saying you're not sorry," I said.

I felt his chest tremble with a little laugh. "How's that working for you?"

I smiled even though he couldn't see my face. "Not so well."

"I guess you *like* being tickled," he said.

"Don't you even think about it," I warned, pulling back from him just a bit.

"We're coming!" he yelled toward the door. I hadn't seen anyone come in, but I turned just in time to see his mom bow out of the room like she hadn't meant to interrupt.

Logan smiled and cocked his head toward the door. "We should go," he said.

Just about the whole family was down at the beach when we got out there. Ryan and I took pictures together by the castle. It was even more remarkable than I remembered, and I caught myself feeling amazed that we had built it. Everyone went on and on about how lucky Ryan was to have a real dentist here to pull her first tooth. It felt great that they were so impressed and thankful, so I didn't mention the tooth was barely hanging on, and that all I had to do was touch it, and it came out.

We stayed down by the beach for a little while, until someone mentioned making an evening pot of coffee and everyone headed toward the house.

"Me and you against Dad and Cody," Evan said, nudging Logan as we approached the house.

"Playin' what?" Logan asked.

"Basketball, dawg," Evan said, puffing out his chest and slapping at it the way guys do.

Logan shrugged. "I'll play to 21," he said.

Evan looked back at Cody, who was holding Ryan on his shoulders.

"I'm in," Cody said.

"What about you, Dad?" Evan asked.

Dan patted his stomach. "Not right after dinner," he said.

"You ate like an hour ago," Evan said. "I think you're just chicken."

"I'm chicken of my heartburn," Dan said, with a fist up to his mouth like he needed to burp.

"What about you, Uncle Rob?" Evan asked.

Logan and Charlotte both looked at their dad who shook his head. "If Dan gets out if it, then I do too."

"I'll play," I said.

Everyone looked straight at me when I said it, and I smiled at their shocked expressions. "Unless girls aren't allowed or something," I added, awkwardly.

"I got her," Logan said.

Cody reached out and pushed at Logan's shoulder. "She's on my team, son. You already said you and Evan were together."

"Yeah, but that's when I thought you were with Uncle Dan or my dad."

"Thanks a lot," Dan said.

"Are you any good?" Evan asked, looking at me.

"I played basketball just about every day of my life from eight-years-old to seventeen."

"She's mine," Cody said.

I held up my hands. "But I am still a girl," I warned.

"I got her," Cody said, bending down to set Ryan on her feet. He looked at Logan. "You already said you were with Evan."

I was being honest when I said I played basketball every day when I was a kid. It was all we had to do most of the time in Kenya. My parents pretty much made us play. It was, after all, cheap entertainment, and it helped all of us get our energy out. When you have forty or fifty kids living in one place, cheap, energy-draining activities are a must. I wouldn't consider myself a huge athlete, but I held my own at basketball, and I felt confident that I could play without completely embarrassing myself.

Mia and Charlotte along with Christy and Dan came down to watch us play. The hoop was mounted on the house near the driveway, and they all sat off to the side as we got started. I was nervous and stiff at first, but the more I got into it, the more I loosened up. I could tell they were playing a little easier on me than they would have been if they were playing with one of the guys, but they'd smile and look impressed when I made a shot or a good pass.

Cody and I ended up barely beating them, but it might have been on account of Logan taking it easy on me a couple of times when he could have done a better job of blocking. Evan gave him a little grief over that, which Logan answered with a nuggie-like wrestling move where Evan ended up in a headlock.

"You can be on my team anytime," Cody said as we all high-fived each other.

"Yeah, I'll bet she can, since Logan lets her score on us all day," Evan said.

"He didn't *let* her do anything," Cody said. "He got scored-on, and that's that."

"Yeah, he just got scored on fair and square," I said, defending myself with the obvious lie.

"I'm just playing around," Evan said, smiling at me. "You did good."

"I know you are," I said. I smiled and tightened my ponytail. "I understand if you can't help lashing out a little when you lose."

Everyone standing around oohed at the wicked burn as Evan laughed and hi-fived me good-naturedly. "You did good," he repeated. "Thanks for playing."

We were all smiling as we started toward the house. Again, Logan and I fell to the back of the pack.

"It's hot that you played basketball with us just now," he said, with a light pinch to my forearm.

I laughed. "Even if you let me win?"

"I couldn't believe you were that good," he said. "Evan was seriously taking it his hardest on you."

"I was not!" Evan said from about three strides in front of us.

"He was!" Logan mouthed, nodding at me.

I giggled. I could feel that my face was flushed with exertion, and I put the back of my hand to my cheeks one-by-one to cool them off.

"I like how basketball looks on you," Logan said.

"Playing it, or blushing from it?"

I glanced at him, and he smiled, but didn't take his eyes from the path in front of us. I found myself staring at his profile. "Both," he said. "They both look good on you. Pulling Ryan's tooth looked good on you, too. I guess you're pretty irresistible no matter what you're doing."

My hunch was that some of the people walking in front of us could hear him, but none of them turned around or acknowledged what we were saying. Logan glanced at me to gauge my reaction, but I just scrunched up my face at him. I was speechless by his compliment, and literally had no idea how to respond. I was afraid I'd say something ridiculous like, "*You're the most irresistible thing I've ever seen, and I think I'm falling in love,*" or "*You're a movie star, but you're also a real person, and I love the real you.*" Yeah, I knew if I opened my mouth, something regrettable would come out of it, so I just didn't.

The smirk I'd been wearing, shifted into a sincere smile, and he reached out to wrap his arm around my shoulder as we walked. I leaned into him, resting my head on his shoulder for a few paces.

"It's been a long day," he said.

I glanced up at him and smiled. "Fun, though."

Chapter 15

The next few days passed quickly. The family constantly had something going on, and I jumped right into the activities. Logan and I spent every waking moment together, but besides the occasional arm around the shoulder or playful pinch, we made no physical contact. He did tickle me one time when I came home from the spa with the girls, and I had my hair styled curly. They were my natural curls, I just always dried my hair straight. He loved what a difference it made, and had chased me around the living room and tickled me that day, but had barely touched me since. I wanted so badly for him to touch me that I was on the verge of "accidently" mentioning being ticklish just to bait him into it.

I had come to love Logan's family during the last few days. Charlotte, Mia, and Paige treated me like I was their sister, and Logan's mom, aunt, and grandma were the sweetest ladies ever. I could see how an environment like this would produce a movie star. They were all positive, upbeat people— go-geters, movers and shakers. They were lovely, sweet, sincere human beings and were all a pleasure to be around.

Everyone asked me questions about Kenya— what it had been like to go up there, and what exactly it was my parents were doing. They all said they'd make donations to the center in the future, and

I knew based on what type of people they were that they'd follow through.

There was no doubt about it—I was falling in love with Logan *and* his family. I was having an amazing time getting to know each of them, and all was all hunky-dory until a few days later when the unthinkable happened.

It was Friday afternoon, and I had gone shopping with Mia and Charlotte. They were still looking around in the store, and I was finished, so I told them I was going to the café next door to get a cup of coffee. I had just left the café with a to-go cup in my hand when a man in a suit walked up to me.

"Are you Rachel?" he asked.

His smile was kind, so I nodded.

"Rachel Stephens?" he asked.

I nodded again, this time looking around curiously.

"Mr. Ritchie has a surprise for you, ma'am," he said, still smiling. "He asked me to pick you up."

I glanced in the direction of the clothing store.

"He's already taken it up with his sister," the man said.

"She knows?" I asked.

"Yes ma'am she does. He said he hoped his sister didn't mention it to you, so he'll be happy to know you were surprised."

"I *am* surprised."

"That was the idea," he said, with a wink.

"So, what do I do?" I asked, feeling butterflies about what Logan could possibly have planned.

"Right this way," he said with a sweeping hand gesture to a sleek black car similar to the one that had brought me to the airport. I followed him, and was about to ask if I could sit in the front like I did with Mike the driver, but he didn't give me the chance. Instead of opening the back door, he went straight for the front, which was fine with me.

"Thank you," I said, smiling as I sat down. "Are you sure they know?" I pointed at the clothing store, and he looked that way with a grin.

"Of course they know. They're probably watching you through the windows right now." He waved in their direction as he closed the door for me.

He turned on the radio, and we drove in silence for two or three minutes before I asked, "Can you tell me where we're going?"

"And ruin the surprise?" he asked, turning the radio down just slightly. We drove for a few more minutes before I asked him his name. He said it was Mike, and I told him how Logan's last driver had been called Mike, too. He asked if they looked alike, and I told him they did a little. We had a good laugh about that, saying it would be funny if all the drivers in the world were named Mike.

We drove out of town. We'd been on a deserted two-lane road for a while when Mike rolled the windows down. It was a nice afternoon, but he was going fast, and the wind caused my long hair to fly all around my face. I was working on holding it back and was about to ask him if he could roll the windows up a little bit when he reached over and snatched my purse out of my lap. Before I knew what had happened, he tossed it out of his window.

"Did you just—" I asked as my head whipped around to look out of the back window of the car. I watched the aftermath of a car in the other lane hitting some object. It swerved and hit the breaks but didn't stop completely before taking off again. Apparently, the person decided whatever they had hit wasn't significant enough to warrant stopping. It was hard to see anything now, but I knew I had just watched the contents of my purse get hit by a car and fly all over the road.

"What in the world are you doing?" I asked, gawking at Mike, the driver.

He adjusted the rearview mirror and took a long look at whatever was behind us.

"What are you doing?" I asked again.

He didn't answer. At first, since I was prone to give people the benefit of the doubt, I thought the whole purse-throwing thing had been an accident, but it was just starting to sink in that I might be in real trouble.

"Where are you taking me?" I asked, looking at the door handle while calculating whether or not I could survive if I jumped out. I looked at him, wondering what would happen if I just jumped on top of him while he was driving.

"I'm dropping you off right up here," he said, as if sensing my panic.

"Why?"

He didn't answer me.

"What's going on?" I asked.

Mike drove without speaking for another minute before doing a reckless U-turn and skidding to a stop on the side of the road. The car was now headed back the way we came and I stared at the empty road wondering what sort of trouble I was in.

"Get out, and lay down with your nose to the ground!" he yelled. His tone was impassive, but I was so scared by the driving, that I wouldn't even think about challenging him, even if he would have asked politely.

It was a narrow street with shallow ditches on each side. I slowly got out and squatted down a few feet from the car.

"Nose to the ground and count to ten!" he yelled. I did as he said, laying belly-down in the grassy ditch.

The instant my nose was to the ground, I heard his tires squeal and felt pieces of debris hit my head and back as he sped off.

I actually counted to ten. The me in a movie would have done something really brave like stand up instantly and chase him down, or at least look up and get his license plate number. But the real me, the scared to death me, counted to ten using the word 'Mississippi' between each number to make sure I wasn't going too fast.

I got to my feet feeling like I was in a dream. I numbly dusted the dirt, sand, and grass off of the front of my chest and legs before focusing on the deserted road ahead of me.

It seemed to go on a thousand miles, and a sick wave of dread flooded my body as I stared at it. I had no phone, no wallet, and no way to know where I was going. I didn't even know the direction of the house. I knew it was on N. Ocean Blvd, but I had no clue about the address. Even if I made it to a phone, I had no one's phone number.

I stood there for several long seconds before making myself take the first step. My only other option was to stand in one place and look shocked, which I obviously wasn't going to do.

I knew we had made several turns after he picked me up, but I hadn't been paying attention to where we were going. I thought we'd been on this road for at least a few minutes before he stopped, so I figured I needed to continue on it for a few miles.

I would have done some sort of math equation to try to figure out the distance since my last turn, but honestly, I had no idea when that was. I hadn't thought anything was wrong until Mike rolled the windows down and tossed my purse out, so I hadn't thought to pay attention to any of that.

I walked a mile or two before I found pieces of my purse. I searched the area for at least twenty minutes. I found my wallet and a few other random things like lip-gloss, but couldn't come up with my phone or the purse itself.

Again, I started walking.

I tried to be positive at first, but I got more and more desperate as minutes stretched to hours. The sun was close to setting when I came to the first promising-looking intersection. I didn't see a sign, but judging from the way the sun was going down, I had a good feeling about taking a left.

Several cars passed me while I was on my journey. One man pulled over and asked if I needed a ride, but I was understandably reluctant and refused even though I desperately wanted to take him up on it.

I thought about a ton of different things as I walked. In my mind, it was obvious that London was the one who had done this. I didn't want to believe it, because the idea of having someone out to get me was terrifying, but I knew deep down it was her doing.

I hated conflict—I did my best to avoid it completely if I could. I wondered as I walked if a life with Logan meant I'd be faced with things like this. I knew paparazzi were a bit of an issue, but I honestly never even considered weird things like this happening. I couldn't believe I had been taken out to the country and dropped off like an unwanted dog.

Who does something like that?

I had to wonder if I was doing the right thing by falling for Logan in the first place. I wasn't looking forward to a life where things like this would happen to me, but then again, I wasn't looking forward to a life without Logan, either. These were the types of thoughts that captured my mind as I walked—I love him, I love him not, type thoughts.

It was nearly dark when I came upon an old country store. The lights were on, but there wasn't a single car in the parking lot. The door dinged when I opened it, and a woman with yellow-y blonde hair came out of the back.

"Hi," she said. She stood behind the register, and instantly began picking at her fingernails like she intended on doing that while I got what I needed.

I stood right in front of her, but couldn't quite find my voice. My throat and mouth were extremely dry. "I was wondering if you know how far it'll take me to walk to the ocean from here," I said finally, after having to cough.

She gave me a skeptical glare, and I smiled at her as best as I could.

"I'm not hurt or anything, but I'm sort of lost without a ride, and I need to make it back to the beach."

She continued to look at me curiously, which made me nervous. "Do you need me to call the police or something?" she asked.

"No," I said, by instinct (though in hindsight, I probably should have let her). "I'm staying with a family on North Ocean, and I need to get back there, that's all."

I couldn't bring myself to explain that someone had just dropped me off in the middle of nowhere. It still didn't seem real.

"North Ocean's pretty long," she said. "So it depends on which end of it you're talking about."

I sighed, helplessly. "I don't remember the address."

She was in the middle of giving me fairly understandable walking directions when a police car pulled into the parking lot. For reasons I don't even understand myself, I felt the urge to run.

"Maybe he can help you," she said as an officer walked in.

I stood really still, looking at him out of the corner of my eye.

"You're not lost are you?" I heard him ask.

I turned slightly to make sure he was talking to me. He was definitely looking at me.

"I'm looking for a young lady who fits your description."

I smiled stiffly. "Depends on who's looking," I said. I knew even as I said it that it was a stupid thing to say, but I was still a little gun shy after the whole Mike the driver, thing.

"I'm looking for someone who belongs to the Hunt family," he said.

"Me!" I said. The word left my lips so quickly that both the officer and the cashier flinched. I raised my hand as I said it, which caused the officer to put a hand on his firearm. I saw him do it and instantly lowered my hand holding my palms up.

"Me," I said, careful to be less excitable this time. "I belong to the Hunts."

"Is your name Rachel Stephens?"

"Yes sir," I said.

I felt palpable relief like a cool breeze going through my veins. I was absolutely overjoyed that someone was looking for me—the Hunts were looking for me.

Chapter 16

The officer introduced himself as Tom Conway and said he'd give me a ride back to the Hunt's place. He didn't ask any questions in front of the clerk. He just thanked her and wished her a good evening, and the two of us walked outside into the warm night air.

The whole time we walked, I planned what I was going to say to him. I could not, for my mother's sake, blame London in any way for this. I knew that would result in my mom losing one of her biggest supporters. *And what if it wasn't even London in the first place?* My stomach turned at the thought of more than one person being out to get me.

"Your family was worried about you," Officer Conway said as we approached his car.

I smiled shyly, telling myself to err on the side of being quiet.

"They were worried there might have been some foul play," he said. "Mind telling me how you ended up on this end of town?"

I gave him a somewhat reluctant expression for a second before changing it to a smile. "I, uh, I don't really know," I said. "I got a ride from someone thinking he was taking me one place, and the next thing I knew, he's dropping me off in the middle of nowhere."

It was the truth, mostly. I just didn't want to get into the whole "pressing charges" thing—especially when I didn't know for sure what had happened.

The officer started to open the car door, but didn't hold it wide enough for me to sit down. "Did you know this person?" he asked, a curious expression crossing his face for the first time.

"No sir."

"But you still got in the car with him?" He was starting to seem a little suspicious, which made me feel anxious.

I took a deep breath, reminding myself that I wasn't a criminal. "I thought he was one of my friend's drivers. He's in movies, and it's common for him to hire drivers. I just rode with one of them the other day in L.A. Anyway, I thought the guy was someone Logan hired, so I got in the car with him."

"And he let you?"

I nodded.

He gave me a skeptical smirk.

"I don't know what happened," I said with a sigh. "Maybe he thought I was somebody else."

"Why didn't you call your friend when you got stranded?"

"Because I didn't have my phone," I said. I picked up my wallet and waved it as if that was proof that I wasn't carrying a phone.

He opened the passenger's door, and I sat on the slick, leather seat. There were so many buttons and lights that I felt like I was in a spaceship. I had no idea how he kept them all straight. There were at least four different types of screens, all displaying various things, including one that was the size of a small flat-screen television and was attached to multiple cameras.

I watched him go across one of the screens as he walked around the front of the car to get into the driver's seat. I took a few deep, calming breaths, and prayed that I'd be able to say the right things. I quit my methodical breathing once I remembered that there were probably cameras recording everything in the car as well. I just sat still and stared out of the front window with what I hoped was a natural half-smile.

Officer Conway got on his phone as soon as he sat down in the car. "Tell Chief Briggs I got his friend's girl," he said with a smile.

I heard some exclamation on the other end, but I couldn't make it out.

"I'm sitting here looking at her."

A pause.

"Out at Lou's store."

Another pause.

"She said she got a ride from the wrong person and ended up stranded. I'm bringing her back to the Chief's friend's house over there on Ocean."

He smiled during the silence.

"You better tell him who found her."

Another smile.

"You're welcome."

He hung up the phone, and put his car into reverse before backing out of the parking lot.

"Someone I know must know the Chief," I said, because I was too nervous to keep quiet like I should have done.

"Diane Hunt," Tom said. "He knew her husband, I believe."

I told myself to be quiet after that, but it was no use. Tom Conway started asking questions and did not stop until we reached Dee-dee's beach house. I answered them as honestly as I could without accusing London Ryder of anything. I gave an account of the car and driver, but I never even mentioned her name.

I had mixed feelings as we pulled up to the beach house. Part of me was happy and relieved to be back, but there was definitely an underlying feeling of shame and embarrassment that it happened in the first place. I didn't know what to expect or how they would react to me disappearing for several hours.

Everyone was out on the front porch when we pulled into the driveway. It was obvious that they had been notified that we were on our way, because they were all out there waiting for us. Everyone else stayed on the porch, but Logan jogged down the stairs as soon as he saw us.

Boy, was he a sight for sore eyes. I had never seen someone so handsome in my whole life. I forgot all about being embarrassed for a few seconds as I watched him fly down the stairs two by two and cross the driveway, headed for the car.

He didn't stand there and wait for me to get out like I thought he'd do. The car was barely stopped when Logan grabbed the door handle and jiggled it. "It's locked from the outside!" Officer Briggs yelled when he saw what Logan was doing. He reached over and pushed a button to unlock it, and Logan pulled at the handle again, this time, succeeding in opening the door.

I barely had my seatbelt off when Logan began pulling me out of my seat. I let out a little squeal at the feeling of being hoisted up so quickly. One second, I was in the police car, and the next, I was wrapped in his arms. I was so relieved; I wanted to cry. My eyes stung with pain of unshed tears, and I blinked hard in an effort to hold them back.

Logan sighed, and his chest rose and fell.

"I can't believe I had to find your girl for you!" Tom Conway called to Logan from the other side of the car. "I thought you were some big time FBI agent."

Logan's chest shook with laughter. "The FBI was about to get called in, don't worry," he said.

"No need for all that," Tom said, confidently. "MBPD's got it under control."

"What happened?" Logan asked, pulling back to look down at me.

"She won't say much about it," Tom said, overhearing Logan's question. "She says she got a ride with someone she thought was your driver and he dropped her off outside of town."

Logan pulled back even further and stared down at me with a confused expression. Some of the family had come off the porch, and were standing closer in an attempt to hear the conversation. I felt exhausted and embarrassed, and I rested my face on Logan's chest.

"I'll tell you about it later," I said where only he could hear.

"I tried to get her to press charges or at least file a report, but she wouldn't," Tom said.

Logan rubbed his hands up and down my upper arms, and onto my shoulders and back. It felt so good that I let out a long sigh. "Why didn't you call?" he whispered.

"I didn't have my phone. I'll tell you everything later."

The officer was star struck by Logan, and ceased asking me questions I didn't want to answer. I had just walked for several miles, and was in a delirious state that had me in a daze. The encounter in the driveway went quickly, and before I knew it, we were headed back inside.

"I think I'll take a shower," I said, looking at Logan as we went in.

He hadn't taken his arm from around me since I'd been back, and I was ever so grateful that he kept it there. The whole family was doing their best to give me space, but I could tell they were curious and had been worried about me.

"I think it was a misunderstanding," I announced before heading up the stairs to take a shower. Logan was standing right beside me and I glanced at him before looking at everyone else with a smile that I hoped didn't seem sad or forced. "Someone tried to give me a ride back to California, and I stopped him before we could get there."

"Someone tried to give you a ride to *California*?" Diane asked as if that made no sense at all.

Ryan cracked up laughing at the thought, and I laughed, knowing it was no use to beat around the bush with this group. "I think maybe someone got their feelings hurt that Logan brought a friend with him and tried to make me leave for a while." I hadn't intended to point any fingers, but the words came out of my mouth before I could stop it.

"Are you talking about London?" Logan asked, pulling back to stare at me.

I shrugged. I looked at him as I spoke, but I knew everyone was listening. You could've heard a pin drop in the room. "It's the only thing I could think of," I said. "I went for a cup of coffee, and a guy approached me saying you'd sent him. He was driving a black car like the one you sent to pick me up the other day, so I thought he was telling the truth. I got in with him and he drove me way out to the country and dropped me off."

"Why didn't you call?" Denise asked. "We would have picked you up."

I glanced away from Logan to look at her. "He sort of threw my phone out the window before he dropped me off."

I heard at least three gasps coming from the women in the room. A few of them even put their hands over their mouths, trying to hide their shock.

"It's fine," I said. "I'm fine. It wasn't really that big of a deal other than I had to walk a little bit."

"And you think that girl might have had something to do with this?" Denise asked.

I shrugged. "I probably shouldn't have said that," I said. "It was just the first thing that came to my mind. Who knows if it was her."

They all looked at me like the whole thing was a crying shame, and I turned to face Logan, who was staring down at me. I just stood there and let his eyes roam over my face. He was making an expression like he was relieved to be staring at me, and I drank it in, breathing easy for the first time in hours. I smiled. "I need a shower," I said.

"I'm going up with you," he whispered.

The others began talking amongst themselves in an effort to give us a little space.

I smiled. "Not in the shower," I whispered.

He knew I was kidding, but his face fell like he was disappointed. "You sure?" he asked. "I was hoping to catch you at a vulnerable time after your trauma."

I let out a laugh. "It wasn't that traumatic."

"Not traumatic enough for me to sneak a shower in there?"

I smiled and leaned into him, resting my face on his shoulder.

"I'm just playing with you," he said with a hand on my head. He absentmindedly rubbed my hairline with his thumb. "I'm just going up to wait for you since I'm not too keen on letting you out of my sight right now."

"I'm keen on your unkeeness," I said.

He shook with silent laughter.

"Just so you know, I knew you were kidding," I said. "I know you don't care about showering with me. You've barely even touched me at all for the last four days."

Logan pulled back and leveled me with an appraising glare. "I hope you're kidding me," he said.

"About what?" I asked, shrugging.

"You know I'm just going slow for *you*, right?" He looked at me sideways.

I smiled and shrugged again. "I didn't know you thought we were going slow," I said. "It felt more like nothing at all."

He tilted his head to the side and lifted his eyebrows at me, causing me to giggle. "What did you just say?" he asked.

I stared down and bit my lip shyly.

He cupped his hand to his ear, and leaned in as if listening closely. "Come again?"

I just continued to giggle.

"Tell me, or you're getting tickled," he warned.

"I said I thought you were doing *nothing*," I whispered instantly to keep from being tickled.

"I'm sorry, I'm confused," Logan said, with a deadpan, dumbfounded expression on his face. "It seems like you're giving me some sort of invitation right now, but I can't quite figure out what it is. Can you rephrase what you're trying to say, in English this time, perhaps."

I smiled and squinted my eyes closed, feeling painfully shy. He put his mouth right next to my ear and said, "I think you're giving me permission to kiss you, Rachel. Am I right about that?"

The warm puffs of air hitting my ear caused a chill to run down my spine.

"Is that what you're saying?" he whispered when I didn't answer right away.

I was helpless to speak, so I nodded.

He had been lightly holding my shoulders, and his grip tightened a little. "You're not just feeling vulnerable right now, are you?"

I shook my head again. "I've been thinking it would happen for days now."

His grip got slightly tighter, and again, he leaned in to put his mouth near my ear. "I thought you needed me to prove something to you."

"I thought you already did," I said.

"Now that I've got official permission, you should know I'm gonna kiss you soon," he whispered. "You won't know when it's coming."

I took a shaky breath, my chest shuttering as it rose.

"Sometime when you least expect it, I'm gonna put my mouth onto yours again." He paused, but I just stood there, trying to act casual like he was whispering normal everyday things into my ear instead of words that made my blood turn warm.

"Is that okay with you?" he asked.

I answered with a nod.

Chapter 17

The remainder of the night was spent torturously waiting for Logan to follow through on his promise.

He came upstairs with me while I took a shower, and then we went back downstairs to hang out with his family. Aside from a few questions right when I first went down there, they were considerate about not putting me on the spot. I told them it was a super weird experience and I was relieved it was over, but I didn't bring up London's name again, and neither did anyone else.

As tradition dictates, the family had a beach bonfire planned for that night. They were going to put it on hold after all my drama, but there was still plenty of time to enjoy it, so they wound up starting it while I was in the shower.

Logan and I met them all at the beach once I got out. Here's where the utter torture part I mentioned comes in… Logan kept his hands to himself for the remainder of the evening! I thought for sure after the conversation we had where I basically gave him a formal invitation to kiss me, that he'd at least go so far as to hold hands or brush up against me or something. It might have been easier to swallow if he didn't look so good, but his masculine frame was comforting and tempting to me, and the firelight caused perfect shadows to dance across his face.

We stayed outside with his cousins, messing around on the beach, throwing a glow-in-the-dark Frisbee, and other fun random stuff like that—we even played a little makeshift game of charades.

They talked about how last year on bonfire night they all went to Travis's party, and how they were glad to spend this year's at home. Mia said she had talked to Travis, but that he was out of town this week on business. Paige told this really romantic story where she and Cody sat in front of this very bonfire for hours talking on their first real night as a couple.

I thought that story might get Logan feeling mushy, but no chance. He told a story when she was done about one time where his friend set his pants on fire at a beach bonfire in L.A. It was a really funny account that had everybody cracking up, but it was far from mushy, and I felt like I could go *crazy* waiting for him to touch me like Cody did to Paige in her version.

It was late at night, and we'd been out there for hours when we decided to call it a night. We all went back to the house at the same time, and this time, Logan and I were walking right in the midst of everyone else instead of falling to the back of the pack. All of the others were in their respective bedrooms when we came in, so we did our best to stay quiet.

Logan pulled at my shirt as we walked through the kitchen. "I'm gonna sleep outside tonight," he whispered. "Evan and Cody wanted to sleep in the hammocks."

I nodded and smiled as if it were of no consequence to me. The other cousins had said goodnight and were off to get ready for bed, but Logan and I stopped in the kitchen to finish our conversation.

"Are you okay up there by yourself?"

"Fine," I said.

"Paige will be up there if she doesn't sleep outside with Cody."

"I'm fine. I was by myself Wednesday night, too. It's not a big deal."

He stepped closer to me, pinning me lightly against the counter. He put his face under my chin and moved it around my neck like he was sniffing around for something. He barely touched me—just got close enough where a part of his face would lightly touch my neck as he shifted. I tilted my chin up, giving him greater access, and hoping he would touch his lips to me. He made this slow, soft motion for what seemed like forever before he put his mouth near my ear.

"I want to kiss you right now more than I've ever wanted anything in my entire life," he said.

I breathed several times before responding. I felt on the absolute edge of some precipice of desire I'd never experienced. "Why are you not doing it?" I asked breathlessly.

He waited several long, agonizing seconds before responding. "I said you wouldn't know when it's coming," he said.

"I thought by that, you meant sometime tonight."

He grinned. "Not necessarily."

"I can't believe you're making me wait," I said.

"Says the girl who wrote the book on waiting."

Logan smiled at me and I smiled back. He pulled back and regarded my face. He inspected it as if he was really taking in every curve and surface.

"I probably have sand on my face," I said, feeling fidgety under his scrutiny.

He shook his head.

I reached up and touched his cheek. He had a few grains of sand stuck in the light row of hair on his jaw, and I used the excuse of dusting it off for a reason to touch him.

"You don't care about that sand," he said, with a sly smile.

I kept using my nails to brush it out. "Yes, I do!" I whispered. With a straight face I said, "I wouldn't be a very good person if I let you go around with sand on your face."

He smiled confidently as he took my hand off of his jaw and wrapped it around himself, placing it on his side.

I could barely breathe. I was so wound up with wanting to touch him that a torso touch was almost too much to handle. I could feel his firm muscles through the fabric of the shirt. I begged myself to pull my hand away, but I couldn't. His hand was over mine, but he was using little to no pressure to hold it there. I could have slipped mine away easily, but I didn't—I couldn't make myself.

"How about there?" He asked. "Do I have any sand there?"

"I'm not really qualified to answer that question," I said.

"Why's that?" he asked. "You could feel it on my face."

"If I start fishing around for sand while my hand's right here, I might start doing and saying things that get me into nothing but a whole lot of trouble."

He smiled before cocking his head to stare into my eyes. "There's a tiger in there somewhere," he said.

I smiled. "Maybe so, but only one man will ever get to see it."

He scrunched his eyes closed as if the temptation was too great. "You know that man's me, right?" he asked.

"That's what you said last September."

"I meant it then, and I mean it now."

"You just don't want to kiss me," I said.

He smiled. "I've already told you I do."

"Then why aren't you?"

"I'm waiting," he said, wearing a teasing grin.

"For what?"

"The right time."

I looked around at the empty room where we were standing.

"It's not right yet," he whispered.

"Why not?"

"Because Cody and Evan are gonna come down those stairs any second." He put his mouth close to my cheek. "You don't know when it's gonna happen." He let his lips touch my cheek for a split second before pulling back. The touch caused me to shiver, which made him smile.

"What if I kiss you first?" I asked.

"You won't," he said.

We smiled at each other. "You're right," I whispered.

"I know," he said.

I was thinking about how I wanted to 'clanch' onto to him and never let go when, just as predicted, Cody and Evan came down the stairs carrying blankets and pillows.

"Sorry to interrupt," Evan said, smiling as they approached us.

"You weren't interrupting anything," I said. "I was just heading upstairs."

"Mia and Charlotte said to tell you to come in their room," Evan said. "Paige is in there, too."

"They're probably painting their nails or piercing ears or something," Cody said.

I turned to head upstairs with a simple smile in Logan's direction.

"Night," I heard him say at my back once I had already turned.

"Night," I said, glancing back at him.

I stopped on the second floor and went to the blue bedroom where Mia and Charlotte were staying. Mia had bought realistic-looking rubber snakes, and was planning on putting one in each hammock with the boys.

There were two obvious flaws with the plan. One was that we'd have to wait till they all fell asleep to do it. And two was that none of us would be out there to enjoy the scare if it, indeed, worked. Mia was dead set on doing it, though, and said she was making it happen with or without us. Of course, we all agreed to help.

We stayed up for an hour before venturing downstairs to the hammocks. They were set up between the piers, so we were walking under the house in sand, and it was easy to be quiet. We had the giggles at first, but once we separated, each going toward our designated victim, we gained composure and got down to business.

Mia got Evan, Paige covered Cody, and I was taking care of Logan. I offered to let Charlotte have him, but she was scared to death, and said I should 'please, please, please' take her place. Charlotte stood near the back of the house like the watchman of the group while the three of us set out to put snakes in hammocks.

191

It was a crazy end to a crazy day, and I was delirious with nerves as I stood next to Logan's hammock. I was trying to make a plan of attack, and hadn't even touched his blanket, when I heard a man's voice yell out a non descript sound.

"Huhhhh!" I heard.

It was only a split second later when the pile of blankets in front of me started to move, and Logan sprang up, throwing his hands in my direction as he made the same "Huhhhh," sound.

He scared the living daylights out of me, and I stumbled backward, falling onto my butt in the sand. Logan was out of that hammock and by my side within seconds. Sure, he was laughing uncontrollably, but he was by my side to give me a hand, nonetheless.

One quick look around told me that the others had suffered my same fate, or similar, at least. I'm relatively sure that while I was stumbling backwards, at least two of them were screaming like we were in a horror movie.

"Evan heard Mia talking about it," Logan said, chuckling as he helped me to my feet. The others were far enough away that I'd been the only one to hear him.

"You're in trouble for this," I said, dusting off my pajama pants.

"Maybe I *like* being in trouble with you."

"Y'all are the absolute worst!" Mia said, loudly enough to get all of our attention. She, too, must have fallen, because she was dusting off her pants when I looked at her.

Evan, Cody, and Logan were still laughing. It must have been a funny sight to see all of us stumbling back like that.

"We're not the ones who were trying to put these things in someone's hammock," Evan said.

I was still holding onto the snake, and Logan reached down to take it from me. He held it out to inspect it even though it was mostly dark. "This looks real," he said. He turned it in his grasp, trying to inspect it. "I'm glad Evan heard them," he said. "This would have freaked me out."

"I know," I said. "I felt bad about doing it. I was thinking about putting yours on the sand underneath you instead."

"That still would have been pretty bad," he said.

"Not as bad as having that in there with you."

"Just so you know for the future," he said. "I'm not a heavy sleeper. There's no way you could have put something under the covers with me without me waking up."

"I was destined for failure," I said morosely.

He smiled. "I'm unprankable."

"Is that a challenge?" I asked.

"It most certainly is!" Mia said, stomping over to snatch the snake from Logan's hand. "We're gonna get 'em if it's the last thing we do. These things were twenty dollars a piece."

"They look real, if it makes you feel any better," Cody said.

I glanced at him just in time to see Mia snatch the one he was holding.

"I know," Logan added. "They're awesome. We'll have to get our dads."

"Oh, don't worry," Mia said. "I'm getting *all y'all*! You never know when. I'm gonna get you when you least expect it."

Logan reached out and pinched at my forearm when she said that, and I looked at him, shaking my head with a smile.

The girls only stayed down there for another minute before deciding to go to bed. We continued dusting the sand out of our pants as we walked into the house.

"We're going to bed," Mia said as we walked inside.

"For sure," I whispered. "I'm tired."

"I'll bet you are," Paige said. She was referring to my ordeal, which had happened earlier that night even though it almost felt like it was a lifetime ago. Paige and I left Charlotte and Mia on the second floor, and continued on to the third. We told each other goodnight as soon as we got up there, and she disappeared into her bedroom.

Chapter 18

I woke up the following morning to Ryan shaking my arm. I blinked, and her precious, smiling face came into focus.

"Hey," I said, sleepily as I sat up on my elbow. I must have been sleeping hard, because it took me a few seconds to realize where I was and who exactly was staring at me.

"Logan said I can use your new selfie stick, but it's still in the box, and my mom and dad said I needed to ask you first."

I was already in a somewhat confused state, and her off-the-wall statement had me racking my brain.

"Ryan Diane, you were supposed to let Ms. Rachel sleep," I heard Paige say from the direction of the stairs.

Ryan and I both glanced in that direction, only I was smiling sleepily, and she was wearing an *I didn't mean to do it* face.

"I'm sorry," Paige said, as she headed toward us.

"It's fine. I was getting up anyway," I said.

I wanted to see what time it was. I leaned over to grab my phone, but remembered once I glanced at the bedside table that I didn't have one. There was, however, a digital clock sitting there, which read 11:28.

"Is it almost noon?" I asked.

Ryan looked at Paige to see if her mom would confirm or deny my question. "You needed the rest after yesterday," Paige said sweetly.

I sat up, feeling dazed and unable to believe I'd slept so late. I blinked at Ryan, doing my best to remember what she'd been asking me when I first opened my eyes.

"I don't have a selfie stick, baby girl, or I'd give it to you," I said in a sleepy tone despite my best efforts to sound awake.

"Yes you do," she said, nodding excitedly. "It's in that bag downstairs. Logan got it for you."

I looked at Paige who nodded and smiled before giving me a regretful expression. "He might have wanted to surprise you," she said. "Sorry. I thought Ryan was coming up to potty."

"I did potty," Ryan said, looking up at Paige. "And then I wanted to see if Ms. Rachel was awake yet." The little girl paused and looked at me. "You were sleeping so much that you didn't even move one inch when we came up here to give you your phone."

"You tried to wake me up earlier?" I asked.

Ryan smiled and nodded proudly. "When Logan wanted to give you your new phone."

"Ryan, Logan might have wanted to surprise Rachel himself," Paige said, quickly cutting in.

Ryan looked back and forth from her mom to me as if calculating whether or not she'd said something wrong, and then she smiled at me, obviously not feeling too bad about letting the cat out of the bag.

"Logan kissed you a bunch, and you didn't even move one single inch!"

My eyes widened, and then I made a silly expression. "You mean to tell me that you let some stinky old boy kiss me when I was sleeping?"

Ryan cracked up laughing, falling onto the couch dramatically. "Logan kissed you right on the mouth, and all you did was..." Ryan trailed off and started open-mouthed breathing like Darth Vader.

I squealed and leaned over to tickle her. "Did I really breathe like that?" I asked, once she stopped laughing.

She nodded.

"Did he say I was snoring?" I asked.

"Nope."

"What'd he say?"

"He said you were pretty. He leaned over and stared at you for a long time, and then he asked me if I liked you or not, and I said yes, and then he kissed you right on the mouth for about five or eight minutes in a row."

"Five or eight *minutes*?" I asked, giggling and tickling her again.

"Yessss!" she said, cracking up.

"Well, I don't know what could possibly be downstairs waiting for me, but just so you know, if I ever *did* have a selfie stick, you'd be more than welcome to use it."

197

"You *do* have one!" Ryan said, grinning from ear to ear. "Remember, I said there's a bag down there with a phone and a selfie stick. I think it's got a case, too."

"Ryan, Ms. Rachel was acting like you didn't tell her in case Logan wanted to surprise her himself."

Ryan stared at her mom, nodding at how that could all make sense, but seeming not to quite understand.

"Let's give her some space to get dressed. She'll come down in a little bit."

"My mom can do your hair if you want to look beautiful," Ryan said.

"She already looks beautiful," Paige said.

"A little spiffing up couldn't hurt," I said, running my fingers through my hair. Paige had already braided everyone else's hair, and until now, I hadn't had the chance to ask her to do mine.

"I'd be happy to braid it for you, if you'd like."

"Could you do two of them coming back like this?" I asked, pulling my sides back.

She smiled and nodded. "Definitely!" she said. "Let me grab a comb and a ponytail holder."

Ryan started jumping up and down like she was about to attend a fashion show.

I changed clothes before Paige braided my hair. I put on some capris with a loose T-shirt layered over a tank, and sat on one of the coffee tables so she could do her thing. She worked quickly, and within minutes, all of the braiding, pinning, and spraying was over, and I was doing the hand mirror in front of a bathroom mirror trick where I was looking at the back of my own head.

"It's so beautiful!" I said. "I can't believe I didn't ask you to do this sooner!"

"I can't believe I didn't ask *you*," Paige said. "Your hair's so pretty."

"Uh-huh!" Ryan said, proudly.

She grabbed my hand and gave me a tug. "So let's go downstairs," she said.

"I've got to brush my teeth and use the restroom, but I promise I'll come down right behind you."

She nodded and took Paige's hand to leave.

I brushed my teeth before putting on some powder foundation and a little mascara along with a super-light layer of lip-gloss. My stomach was churning at the thought of Logan buying me a phone. *Who was I kidding?* I was barely even thinking about the phone. It was the kiss that was on my mind—the kiss I hadn't even known about, the one that happened while I was sleeping.

I stared at myself in the mirror as I rubbed my lips together to spread the lip-gloss. I imagined Logan's lips on mine for five or eight minutes straight while I slept, and I smiled at the thought of Ryan trying not to giggle when he kissed me.

I breathed one long sigh to work up the nerve to go down there and see everyone, and off I went.

"Here it is!" Ryan said, as I came into the living room downstairs. Paige was in the kitchen talking to

Diane, but besides the three of them, there was no one else around.

"We need to bring it outside and let Logan give it to her," Paige said.

"Where's is Logan?" I asked.

"Everybody's down at the beach," Paige said. "We just came up so little miss sunshine could potty."

"I'm headed down there, too," Diane said.

"You can come with us, Dee-dee," Ryan said.

Diane smiled. "I think I just might."

Ryan came up to me holding the bag. It was from a major cell phone carrier, and my first thought was wondering if he'd already been to the store this morning. Then, my second thought was whether or not famous people did their own shopping. Maybe he had someone else go get it for him and deliver it to the house. I stared at the bag in my hand for a few seconds, contemplating peeking inside.

"Is this really for me?" I asked, looking at Diane and Paige.

They both nodded, but it was Diane who spoke up. "Logan felt terrible about what happened yesterday," she said. "He and Evan went out this morning and came back with that. You can take it to the beach so he can see you open it if you want."

I nodded as I rolled the top of the bag closed so I wouldn't be tempted to look. Diane thrust a mug of coffee into my hand when I came into the kitchen, and we all set out for the shore.

It was a beautiful day, and the whole family was outside enjoying it. Some were sitting on chairs, others on towels, and a few were in the water. It didn't take me long to spot Logan, who was in the water with Charlotte and Cody. He smiled and started heading toward us the moment our eyes met. I watched as he swam to the shore, and walked out of the water, taking my breath away with his long, confident stride.

Did I mention that he didn't have a shirt on?

He didn't. He reached up and used his hand to shake the water out of his hair and off of his face, smiling the whole time he approached. I took an unsteady breath as I watched. *Forget about taking a sip of that coffee. It was all I could do to breathe.* We smiled at each other as the distance between us closed. I knew the whole family was out there, but I could see no one but Logan.

"You got it?" he asked gesturing to the bag.

I held it up. "No," I said, innocently. "They said it might be for me, but I didn't see what was inside."

"Open it," he said.

He came to stand near me, and once again, I felt speechless. Droplets of water covered his perfect body, and I couldn't help but look at him. I tried not to stare, but my gaze kept returning every time I glanced away.

"It's not wrapped or anything," he said, reminding me what I was supposed to be doing.

I smiled and handed him my coffee mug. He took a sip of it the instant he had it in his possession, and for whatever reason, that made me smile. I liked him drinking out of my cup.

I looked in the bag to find a box with the newest, most expensive iPhone on the market. My old phone had been one of those, just not nearly as new or as much memory. There was, indeed, a selfie stick in the bag, along with a leather case for the phone.

I stared into the bag for nearly a full minute before looking at him. "What is this?" I asked, even though I knew good and well what it was.

He smiled. "It's a fishing lure," he said, with a deadpan expression.

I narrowed my eyes at him. "Why'd you get me a phone, Logan?"

"Because you needed one," he said, chuckling.

"Yeah, but it's not your job to buy me one," I said.

He held his hand to his chest as if I had just stuck a dagger into him. "Ouch," he said.

"I mean you didn't have to—" I cut the statement short when he grabbed my arm and pulled me into his arms. We were both holding things, and he was soaking wet, so it was slightly awkward, but I snuggled up to him as smoothly as I could.

"Go put your coffee and your phone over there and come out into the water with me," he said.

"I don't have my swimsuit on," I said.

"So? People swim in shorts and a T-shirt all the time."

I stared at him, unable to imagine how I ended up at the ocean with a movie star.

"Go," he said, pinching my side.

I giggled as I walked toward the chairs where his mom was sitting.

"Can you open it now?" Ryan asked as I passed.

"I sure can," I said. "I stopped and fished around in the bag till I came up with the selfie stick. I took it out of the packaging and handed it to Paige, holding my bag up in the process. "I'm putting this right here. Just come dig in it if you need instructions or whatever."

"Thank you!" Paige said, almost apologetically.

I gave her a smile that said she really shouldn't be worried about it.

My hair was half-up in Paige's beautiful braids, but I pulled the rest of it back into a low bun as I walked toward the water. Logan was already waist-deep in it, and I smiled as I walked out there to meet him. He backed up as I approached, and by the time we connected, I was almost up to my chest in it.

"You're getting me soaked," I said.

"What? I told you I wanted you to swim with me."

"I thought you meant like up to our knees or whatever."

He smiled wryly at me. "That's not swimming."

The gentle waves hit against us, coming almost up to my shoulders when they peaked. I jumped when a particularly large one came, and Logan caught me and pulled me into his arms. My clothes were soaking wet, and I didn't care at all. I stood on his feet, and got up on my tiptoes, giving me a height advantage that almost put us eye to eye. I giggled and shifted as a few waves rolled by and hit our shoulders.

"You can't buy me a cell phone," I said.

He didn't say anything; he just smirked at me like I was being silly.

"That's too much," I insisted.

He just continued to stare at me with an adorable grin.

Truth was, I was relieved to have the gift. Eventually, I'd be making decent money, but I wasn't quite there yet, and I happened to need a phone. Besides, I could tell by the way Logan was looking at me that he was going to make me keep it even if I tried to give it back. So instead of refusing it, I humbly said, "Thank you."

Chapter 19

Logan continued to hold me by the waist as we rose and fell with the waves.

"Don't worry, my number's already programmed in there," he said.

I smiled at him. "I'll make sure to call you once I get it turned on."

"It's already on," he said. Then he answered my curious glance with, "I had it activated when I bought it."

He was so matter of fact when he said it that I almost just smiled and nodded as if that was a normal statement.

"How'd you get my account?" I asked, once I figured out that it wasn't.

"It's on my plan," he said.

"Why?" I asked.

"Don't worry, I got them to keep your same number. You lost all your contacts, though. Except for me. I'm in there."

"How'd I end up on your plan?" I asked.

He smiled. "Because I put you there."

We both jumped to avoid getting hit in the face with an especially big wave.

"Why'd you do that?" I asked.

His smile was so wonderful that I almost forgot what we were talking about.

He shrugged as he glanced toward the incoming waves. "Because I figured you'd end up on there anyway," he said. "I didn't see a point in putting it off."

"Logan, why would you put me on your cell phone account," I asked, feeling like one of us needed to be practical.

"I just told you," he said. "I knew you'd end up on there anyway."

"What, like if we would get married or whatever?"

My whole body buzzed with nerves as I said the word 'married'. I regretted it the instant it left my mouth.

"*When* we get married," he said, smiling irresistibly.

"Logan, who knows how long that'll be. You can't just—"

He cut me off, saying, "*We* know how long it'll be. We're the ones who decide that."

I smiled and narrowed my eyes at him. "You know what I mean," I said. "It's not like we're getting married tomorrow or anything."

"We could."

Oh goodness, how I wished that were true. I would marry this man in a heartbeat. There was just no way. I shot him another narrow-eyed smirk, which he answered with a smile.

"What?" he asked.

"You're being silly."

"I am not."

"So we just decide to get married, and we run right out and do it?" I asked.

"Yep," he said. "As the bride and groom, it's pretty much up to us."

"And I'm supposed to assume you think it's a good idea," I asked.

"Yes, I do."

"And then what? We have it annulled the next morning and shave our heads before we head back to California?"

He ran a hand through his closely-cropped hair, causing tiny droplets of water to spray all over the place. I squinted and flinched, and he shook more vigorously, causing me to giggle.

"It's a no to the annulment, and I like your hair right where it is." He looked at my head as if trying to imagine what it'd look like short. "Although, I'm sure you'd look fine with it shaved."

Waves continued to hit us as we swayed to the gentle rhythm of the ocean. I put my mouth near his ear. "Logan," I whispered with my hand on his bare chest. "It seems like you're talking marriage with me right now."

"I am."

"Why?" I asked.

"Because I want to marry you, Rachel."

I was weightless in the water, which was a good thing because my knees were weak.

"When?" I asked.

"Soon."

"Are you saying this because of what I told you about waiting till I get married?"

"I'm saying it because I want to marry you," he said, still smiling. He regarded me sweetly before he said, "Rachel, you should know how thankful I am that you've waited. I can't tell you how much it means to me to know I'm the only man who'll ever know you like that."

Statements like that made me feel like he was serious and this was actually happening. My heart started beating a million miles an hour.

"Do you want to marry me?" he asked.

I smiled and bit my lip as I nodded shyly.

"You love me?" he asked.

I nodded again.

"See?" he said. "Why'd you even ask about that dang-old phone?"

I laughed.

Our eyes locked and we stared at each other for several long seconds as the ocean continued to pulse.

"Are you asking me to marry you right now?" I asked, squinting at him.

He kept one around my waist and put the other hand behind my head. "Rachel," he said, pulling me against him. "Close your eyes for a second."

I didn't hesitate. I rested my face on the top of his chest, closing my eyes in the process. He held me to him, bobbing as waves continued to it us.

"Pretend we're somewhere with all of our friends and family members. Your mom, and dad, and brother are there, along with the people you love from the center, and your friends and family from California. All my people are there, too—everybody who's here with us now, plus my crew out in L.A. It's about a hundred or so people, probably. And we're somewhere really cool—some place that was really thoughtful of me to consider."

"Like the hillside in Santa Barbara."

"Exactly," he said.

I could hear the smile in his voice.

"So we're all at the bench—you, me and everyone in the whole world that we love."

"Then what happens?" I asked.

"Then I give a really charming speech about how we first met and kissed there."

"Are you telling the part about me making you wait till September?"

"Do you want me to tell it?" he asked.

I shook my head without opening my eyes.

"No? Okay, I won't tell it, then. I say we lost touch, but that I knew the whole time that I'd find you again. I talk about all the things I love about you, and then I pull a gigantic, custom-made diamond ring—"

He stopped talking when I shook my head.

"A tasteful, but moderately big diamond—"

I shook my head again.

"Something super simple and give the rest of the money I was gonna spend on it to your parents' center."

I squeezed him to let him know he got it right that time, and he laughed before continuing.

"Then I say, Rachel, I love you. I want to be with you for the rest of your life. I want to eat sushi, and play basketball, and have babies, and visit Kenya, and do all the other things you do when you're married and in love. I want to marry you!"

I could feel even with my eyes closed that he was gesturing somehow with his hands behind my back. "I'm asking you right here in front of all of our friends and family, Rachel..." he cleared his throat. "Dr. Rachel Stephens," he corrected. "Will you marry me?"

He squeezed me when I didn't respond right away. I had my eyes closed, basking in the story, and didn't realize he wanted me to actually respond.

"Will I marry you?" I asked, peeking up at him.

He was smiling at me. "Don't leave me hanging on this hillside full of people," he urged, causing me to giggle.

"Are you asking in the story, or right now?"

"Both," he said.

"I'm saying yes to that."

"In the story, or right now?"

I pulled back far enough to focus on his face. "Both," I said.

"Okay, then just imagine that I'm slipping the ring on your finger."

I closed my eyes, as if imagining it.

"There's only one problem," I said.

"What is it?"

"I don't want to imagine anymore."

"Why not?"

"Because the story's not as good as reality."

His grip tightened, and he held me close. "You're saying you liked being all alone with me out here in the ocean instead of me giving a big speech in front of a bunch of people?"

"I love it."

"You're saying this right here is better than some long, thought-out thing?"

I nodded and looked around, taking in our surroundings. My gaze shifted from the scenery to Logan's chiseled, leading-man face.

"It's pretty perfect," I said.

"Even without the ring?" he asked.

I nodded.

He smiled at me like he knew something I didn't.

"What?" I asked.

"Sometimes you won't have any say in what I buy you," he said.

"What's that mean?" I asked.

"It means sometimes I get to spend a little money on you—not on the charity of your choice, but on *you*."

"What exactly are you saying?"

"I'm saying you probably won't have a say in what sort of ring I choose."

"Why not?"

He looked as if he might say something, but instead, he took my hand and put it on the side of his leg.

"Is there a ring in this pocket?" I asked, the instant it sunk in what he was doing.

He smiled and nodded at me.

I was too nervous to dig for it, so I lifted my hand out of the water, and covered my eyes instead. Seconds later, Logan's hand came out of the water holding a loose diamond ring. It dripped and I remember thinking, *thank goodness that thing didn't fall out of his pocket.*

It was simple in its design, but there was a more-than-moderately-sized solitaire sparkling in the sunlight. It was the most beautiful thing I'd ever seen, and it was mine. I couldn't wait to get it on my finger. I gingerly took it from him and tried it on. I stared at it for several seconds, unable to believe any of this was really happening.

"There's just one thing we're missing," I said, finally.

Logan didn't respond right away, but I just stood there waiting for him to figure out what I meant. The corners of his mouth curved upward into a slow grin.

"I know what it is," he said.

"You do?"

"Yep."

"You must not," I said.

"Why?"

"Because you're not doing it."

I stared at his mouth—not because I was trying to give him a hint of what I wanted to happen, but because I couldn't look away from it. It was beckoning to me. I smiled at the thought.

"I have no idea what you're talking about," he said, making me squirm in his arms.

"Will you please..." I said. I trailed off before I could say will you please *kiss me*. It was obvious that I had changed my mind and decided to cut my question short, and he smiled because of it.

"Will I please what?"

"You know what," I said.

"Why don't *you* do it?" he asked.

"Because I want you to do it first," I said.

"What do you want me to do?" he asked, but even as the words left his mouth, he took my hands in his and placed them on the sides of his own face. I kept my hands there when he dropped his arms to wrap them around my waist again.

"Now use your hands to pull my face toward you," he said.

I did as he instructed, pulling gently down on his face until only an inch or two separated us. "What now?" I whispered breathlessly.

He slowly brought his lips to mine. It seemed like they'd never make contact, but once they did, it caused an electrical impulse to resonate through my body. Our lips were only touching for a few seconds when I pulled him closer. I leaned into him at the same time, deepening the kiss considerably. I never really let myself go too far with guys, so deep kisses were sort of unknown territory for me. Logan's tongue entered me in a way I'd never felt before. The hot, wetness of it caused waves of some new desire to wash over me. The ocean's waves continued to rise and fall around us, making the experience that much more surreal. Logan kissed me like he meant it. He kissed me like he'd been waiting since last September to do it. I surrendered to him, fully trusting that he had nothing but pure intentions toward me. I let him invade my mouth—let us both give over to the feeling of it, knowing there was more to come once we were married.

I must have gone dumb and blind with passion for a few seconds, because by the time Logan broke the kiss, my legs were tangled around his, and I had no recollection of putting them there.

"Logan?" I said, my lips still almost touching his.

"Huh?"

"I think it's gonna be fun once we get married."

He smiled. "It's gonna be real fun, kitty cat."

He glanced over my shoulder, and I turned to find Cody walking toward us. It took him a minute, but eventually he made it out to where we were standing.

"I hate to interrupt, but I just wanted to give you a head's up that there's someone with a camera about a hundred yards that way."

Logan squinted in the direction that Cody indicated, but didn't seem to care much. He shrugged and washed his face with a handful ocean water. "It's fine," he said. "They're gonna be sick of seeing us together before long."

"We just thought we should tell you since you know, you two were..."

"We're getting married," Logan said.

"Really?" Cody asked.

"I asked her just now on a sentimental hillside in front of all our friends and family, and she said—"

Logan trailed off at the sight of me shaking my head.

"I asked her just now when we were all alone out here in the ocean, and she said, 'yes'," he amended.

I smiled and nodded at him as I brought my hand to the surface of the water for Cody to inspect.

He stared down at it before lifting his eyebrows at us with a smile. "Does Aunt Denise know?" he asked.

Logan shook his head. "No, I'll tell everybody when we come up in a minute."

"When are you doing it?" Cody asked.

"Yesterday," Logan said.

"Soon," I said, smiling.

"Soon," Logan agreed.

"I guess I'll be the first to congratulate you, then," Cody said. He smiled at me. "The family already loves you." He motioned to the shore. "They're up there talking about how many of us can take a trip to Kenya in a few weeks."

I felt speechless, so I just smiled at him and blew a kiss to him and then one to everyone on the shore even though none of them were paying attention to us.

"I'll leave you two alone, I just wanted you to know about the photographer."

"I'm glad we have pictures of it," Logan said, smiling down at me. "He's doing us a favor."

Cody turned and dove into the water, swimming away.

"What if he missed the kiss?" I asked.

"Who? The photographer?"

I nodded.

Logan shook his head disapprovingly. "That would be terrible, he said. And just like that, his lips were on mine again. He shifted so we were facing a different direction. "We gotta make sure he gets a good one," he said, barely bothering to take his lips off mine when he spoke. This made the words come out muffled, which sounded so sweet.

I wanted his lips on me forever.

"I love you, too," he said, once he pulled away.

"How'd you know I love you, one?" I asked.

"I just know," he said.

"You're right."

Epilogue

Three weeks and two days later.
Nairobi, Kenya.

"I can't believe this is happening," my mother said, as she adjusted the white, birdcage veil that was hanging over my face.

My soon to be sister and mother-in-law had taken me shopping for the veil and dress while we were in L.A. They helped me choose something elegant, yet simple enough to fit with getting married at a farm in Africa.

Logan flew twenty people out for the wedding— some from L.A., and some, of course, from Carolina. All of them knew that it was a combination wedding and work trip, and everyone seemed excited about helping out at the center while they were there.

Logan's publicist had leaked just enough about the wedding plans so that the news wouldn't come as a complete shock to his fans. The photo of our rendezvous in the ocean made the press instantly, and Logan came out right away, saying he'd known me for a while and his intention was to marry me.

Long story short, it was happening.

Right now, on this very day.

Today, I would become Mrs. Rachel Ritchie. And tonight... well, let's just say I was a little nervous but mostly excited about tonight.

"I can't believe it's happening, either," I said. "The farm looks so beautiful. Thank you for doing all this."

My mom put her hand on my forearm. "You look beautiful, sweetheart." She gave my arm a squeeze. "You know I'm picky about my baby girl, and I just wanted to let you know how much I love Logan."

"He's a good one, isn't he?"

My mom smiled and nodded. "I love his family, too. And your dad and brother feel the same way."

I smirked at her. "Cub especially loves having Charlotte and Mia around."

She winked at me. "That might be a little perk for him." Her smiled turned sincere as she rubbed my arm again. "Your dad and I couldn't be happier for you, Ray."

"I'm happy, too." I said. "And I'm so glad I get to do it here with you guys."

"Are you ready?" my dad asked, peeking his head into the farmhouse. "I think it's time."

My dad walked my mom to her seat before coming back to get me. I walked barefoot on the tan soil path that ran through the grass just as I had done as a child.

Everyone had chipped in to set up a beautiful, rustic scene where the guests were sitting in small groups on blankets. Logan was standing at the other end of the courtyard waiting for me. My eyes met his, and instantly, I wanted to cry. I got that aching feeling in my jaw, along with burning eyes. I took a deep breath.

"You okay, honey?" my dad asked.

"Better than ever," I whispered.

He squeezed my arm, and patted my hand. "I'm proud of you."

I glanced at him with a smile before turning to face Logan again. We stared at each other while I approached, both knowing we were about to do the right thing.

My dad shook Logan's hand before handing me over to him. The whole exchange felt so symbolic, it was like I was in a dream.

"I love you," Logan whispered.

"I love you too," I said.

My veil wasn't long at all. It barely reached my chin, and all Logan had to do to access my mouth was lift the edge of it slightly with his fingertip. He pulled me in with one hand while he lifted my veil with the other. Before I knew what was happening, he kissed me. This obviously took me by surprise, but I loved him so much that I went with it. It seemed, after all, as good a time as any to kiss him.

Some people whooped, and hollered, and whistled from the audience.

"That's supposed to happen after the ceremony," Evan shouted. I knew it was Evan; I could tell by his voice.

We both smiled as we broke the kiss. We stared at each other as we pulled back, not caring about anyone else. Finally, we faced my dad who had not only walked me down the isle, but was now also officiating the ceremony.

Several more whistles came from the audience, prompting Logan to lean over and do it again.

"That's all, I promise," Logan whispered after a few more stolen kisses.

"Till later," I said.

His eyes widened like it was the first time he had considered the possibility.

We were both smiling as we turned to say our vows.

It was a perfect wedding.

The farm was charming and beautiful, and our families were there. Logan was mine, and I was his, and there was no doubt in our minds that it was supposed to be that way.

The End
(till book 3)

Hugs and many thanks to my awesome team Chris, Jan, and Glenda.

CPSIA information can be obtained at www.ICGtesting.com
Printed in the USA
LVOW08s1727201016

509596LV00004B/766/P